D0244301

The Secret Life of
Sally Tomato

C0000 002 527 108

Also by Jean Ure

Boys Beware
Sugar and Spice
Is Anybody There?
Secret Meeting
Shrinking Violet
Passion Flower
Pumpkin Pie
Skinny Melon and Me
Becky Bananas, This is Your Life!
Fruit and Nutcase
The Secret Life of Sally Tomato*
Boys on the Brain
Family Fan Club

and for younger readers

Dazzling Danny
Daisy May
The Monster in the Mirror

Also available on tape, read by John Pickard

The Secret Life of Sally Tomato

JEAN URE

Illustrated by
Karen Donnelly

HarperCollins *Children's Books*

First published in Great Britain by HarperCollins *Children's Books* 2000
HarperCollins *Children's Books* is a division of HarperCollins*Publishers* Ltd
77-85 Fulham Palace Road, Hammersmith,
London W6 8JB

The HarperCollins *Children's Books* website address is
www.harpercollinschildrensbooks.co.uk

10

Text copyright © Jean Ure 2000
Illustrations copyright © Karen Donnelly 2000

ISBN-13   978 0 00 675150 2

The author and illustrators assert the moral right to be
identified as the author and illustrators of this work.

Printed and bound in Great Britain by
Clays Ltd, St Ives plc

Conditions of Sale
This book is sold subject to the condition
that it shall not, by way of trade or otherwise,
be lent, re-sold, hired out or otherwise circulated
without the publisher's prior consent in any form
of binding or cover other than that in which it is
published and without a similar condition
including this condition being imposed
on the subsequent purchaser.

Mixed Sources
Product group from well-managed
forests and other controlled sources
www.fsc.org   Cert no. SW-COC-1806
© 1996 Forest Stewardship Council

FSC is a non-profit international organisation established to promote the
responsible management of the world's forests. Products carrying the FSC
label are independently certified to assure consumers that they come
from forests that are managed to meet the social, economic and
ecological needs of present and future generations.

Find out more about HarperCollins and the environment at
www.harpercollins.co.uk/green

For Henrietta
(We made each other laugh)
and for my friend
Mark Alexander
(also known as Ranny Arbuckle...)

Some people keep diaries: I am going to keep an alphabet! I am going to do two letters a week, starting from Monday. (The beginning of the spring term.) For every letter, I am going to write a poem. Some of them may be quite rude; it depends how I'm feeling. In between the poems I shall write down chunks of everyday life. *My* life! All the things that are happening to me, and especially with girls. If by the time I reach Z I still have not done it, I shall most probably go out and shoot myself.

Or drown myself, as I don't have a gun.

Or swallow fifty-eight bottles of aspirin, or hurl myself madly in front of a train, or tell Kelvin Clegg he's a dork and get myself totalled.

I have got to have done it before then!

When I say *done it*, I mean kissed someone.

When I say *someone*, I mean –
a girl!

When I say *kiss*, I mean – **KISS!**
Not just a peck on the cheek.
Though as a matter of fact, I haven't even done that.
I am twelve years old and I haven't even pecked a
girl on the cheek!

I am seriously worried that there may be
something wrong with me. It surely can't be normal
to have reached the age of twelve and never kissed a
girl? Even Bones has done it! He's done it twice.
The first time was with his cousin Jemma, who is
rather forward and actually kissed *him*, so he
couldn't make the most of it.

The second was with Nasreen Flynn, at Juniors. They were alone in the classroom, being Tidiness Monitors, and he made a grab at her and she didn't resist.

I asked him what it was like and he said it was like pressing your lips against a ripe peach. I could try asking Mum if she'll buy some peaches so that I can practise, but it's not the same as the real thing. How come Bones gets to do it and not me?

Answer: because he is *normal*. That's why. My sister calls him Bullet Head, and I don't think he's what most girls would consider hunky as he is quite short and squat and has a face like a beaming garden gnome but he obviously exudes manliness in great quantity. His hormones rage and froth. When he sees a girl he's like a wild beast, with this uncontrollable urge to kiss and grapple.

I don't seem to have any hormones. Or if I do, they don't seem to be working properly.

I hope I'm not gay! Except I don't see how I can be because if I was gay I would fancy Bones, which I most definitely *do not*.

Unless I fancy him without knowing it???

This is frightening! Why can't I be the same as other people?

Yesterday I bumped into Kelvin Clegg and his mates as I was on my way to Bonesy's. Kelvin called out, "Whey-hey, it's Sally Tomato!" and they all sniggered. I know they only do it because of my name being what it is, and because of Kelvin Clegg having the mental age of a retarded flea and thinking he is being amusing. I know this. All the same, I sometimes can't help wondering if they sense something? These Neanderthal types often do. They're like dogs, they can sniff things out.

This is a list of the things I feel are abnormal about me:

1. My name. Salvatore d'Amato. Salvatore! I ask you! It's ridiculous. I don't even speak Italian! Nobody in the family speaks Italian. It's like some kind of sick joke. OK if you're living in Rome or somewhere, but I'm not! I'm living in London, five minutes away from Kelvin Clegg, who calls me Sally Tomato.

When I'm not being called Sally, I'm being called Sal. It must have a psychological effect. Parents can be very cruel to their offspring in their choice of names. Like Mr and Mrs Cart, who christened their baby Orson.

I'd rather be Orson Cart than Sally Tomato!

2. The second thing that is not normal about me: I am not into sports. Only swimming, and that doesn't count. Not at our school. The only thing that counts at our school is football. Well, and bashing people if you happen to be Kelvin Clegg.

3. The third thing: I read a lot of books. That's a really nerdy sort of thing to do. My sister hasn't read a book in years. She's more interested in boys. Dad says she's obsessed with boys. She's almost super-normal!

4. The fourth naff thing about me: I write poetry.

That is even more nerdy than reading books. It is so nerdy that I have never told anyone, not even Bones.

5. I am scared of heights.

6. I am scared of getting a brain tumour.

and

7. This is one I have just thought of. A few weeks ago I saw *Lassie Come Home* on television and I cried. My sister cried, too, but that is all right because she is a girl. Even though she is fourteen, she is allowed to cry. Boys are not supposed to.

What is the matter with me???

If it turns out that I am truly as abnormal as I fear, it will be all my parents' fault. My parents are seriously weird. But seriously. I mean, Dad! *A dentist.* Only a warped personality would choose to become a dentist.

And Mum. A housewife! How could I tell anyone that my mum is a housewife? They wouldn't know what I was talking about. It's like something out of the Dark Ages! Other people have mums that are marine biologists or bank managers or work in Tesco's. Why can't I?

Mum says she hasn't got time to do any of those things, she's too busy with her classes. Last year she took classes in car maintenance and reflexology. This year it's vegan cookery and antiques. She keeps making all these gungy dishes like carrot and oatmeal pudding and stuffed cabbage leaves. When she's not doing that she's rushing off to car boot sales to look for genuine antique junk.

I guess it's no more than you can expect of someone that married a dentist. If she wasn't weird before, she's become weird since.

She's quite nice; so's Dad. I don't dislike them or anything. But I do think they are weird! Bones's dad is a long-distance lorry driver and his mum works at B&Q. That's what I call normal.

It's why Bones is normal and gets to kiss girls and I don't. But I intend to! I have made up my mind. I mean this most sincerely! It is my project for this term.

– to work on getting to know girls better

– if possible, to acquire an actual girlfriend

– if I can't do that, then at least kiss one, preferably Lucy West, but if I can't get her then I wouldn't mind Emma Crick or Carrie Pringle.

– if all else fails I will make do with Nasreen Flynn, though I would rather not kiss one that has already been kissed by Bones.

By the time I reach Z, I might have kissed them all!

A, B, C, D
Here I come!
Swifter than the wind
From a polecat's bum!

A is for armpit,
Which smells when you're hot.
Specially great hairy ones.
They smell A LOT.

You can check whether your armpit smells by holding up your arm and burying your nose in it. Your armpit, I mean. I have done this. I could not detect any odour.

It is very important not to have odour if you want to kiss a girl. Girls are into cleanliness in a big way. At least, they are if my sister is anything to go by. She spends for ever in the bathroom. Dad gets really mad at her. Sometimes he yells.

"Have you become a permanent fixture?" he goes. "There are other people in this house besides you, you know!"

The other morning, at breakfast (after Dad had been yelling) I asked her what she did in there. I wasn't being nosy; it was serious research. I am trying to learn all I can about girls and their habits.

My sister gave me this really poisonous look, like

I was some kind of noxious bug, and snarled, "Don't you start!"

I said that I wasn't starting. "I just want to know what you do!"

"Do you really need to ask?" said Dad, fanning the air. "I'm surprised they let you into school smothered in that muck."

"It *happens* to be *perfume*," said Iz.

"Where do you put it?" I said. I like to be clear about these things. "All over? Or just—"

"Oh, go jump in a bucket!" said Iz. "You get on my tits!"

She doesn't have any tits, so I don't know how I was supposed to have got on them. An ant couldn't get on her tits, hardly.

My sister is obviously just as weird as the rest of the family. Yesterday I asked Mum if she thought she was quite normal.

"Your sister?" she said. She sounded surprised. Like, why would I ask such a thing?

"I was just wondering," I said, "if all girls were like her."

Mum sighed and said, "Unfortunately."

"Why unfortunately?" I said.

"Well… it's a phase they go through," said Mum.

"All of them?"

"Most of them."

"Like about… how many?"

"About 99.9%. Why?"

I explained that I was making a study of them. For some reason Mum seemed to think this was amusing. She said, "And what have you discovered so far?"

I said, "Well, I've discovered that they like to be clean."

"Really?" said Mum. "What made you come to that conclusion?"

"Observation," I said. "Taking a million hours in the bathroom."

Mum laughed. I think it is what is called a *hollow* laugh.

"They don't go into the bathroom to get clean!"

"So what do they go in there for?" I said. "Just to splosh perfume over themselves?"

"Oh, more than that," said Mum. "Far more than that! It's a total experience… it's a *happening*. They look at themselves… all over, from every angle. They agonise over spots and whether their noses are too big or their mouths are too small. They use their dad's razor to shave their legs – and don't bother to clean up after themselves. They drench the place in talcum powder. Their *mother's* talcum powder. They snip bits off their hair and block the plug hole. They cut their toenails in the hand basin. They *varnish* their toe nails in the hand basin. They drop great blobs of it and ruin the enamel, thus making their mums and dads extremely angry. They—"

Mum broke off. "What else can I tell you?"

I said, "Um... well! They do wash a bit, I suppose?"

"I don't know about washing. They have hot baths and stay in there for hours on end, wasting water and putting up their parents' water bills."

"It'd make them pretty clean, though," I said, "wouldn't it?"

"It might make their *bodies* clean," said Mum. "The state of their bedrooms, on the other hand, leaves a very great deal to be desired!"

I don't know why she brought bedrooms into it. She sounded kind of bitter. But at least I have learnt a few more things about girls.

This afternoon when I got home an old friend of Mum's from school had arrived. She is staying with us over night. When she was at school she was called Match, as she was extremely thin. She is still called Match even though she is now extremely fat. She and Mum seem to think this is very funny and giggle a lot.

The fat Match person has not seen me since I was little. She said to Mum, "My! Hasn't Sal shot up? He'll be quite a lady killer when he's filled out."

"You reckon?" said Mum.

"Oh, yes," trills the fat Match. "He's going to be a real charmer!"

My sister was there and she made this loud vomiting noise. As far as she is concerned, I am just something that has been brought into the house on the bottom of a shoe. Any feeling of triumph I may have had, however, was short-lived. The next thing to come out of this person's lips completely destroyed me.

"He looks such a nice young lad!"

To which my sister went, "Hah!"

This is extremely disturbing. I don't want to look like a nice young lad! I want to look sultry and degenerate.

I am still worried that I may be gay and not know it. Kelvin Clegg keeps referring to me as Sally Tomato. Even Bonesy sniggers.

B stands for boob and also for breast.
As letters go, it's one of the best!
It's also for babe and for bust and for bra
Plus in addition of course there are:
Backside and bottom and bosom and bum
And some which would certainly not please
your mum!

A nice young lad would not write a poem like that. And three massive cheers! I can forget about being gay! I fancy Lucy West like crazy. She is the one for me! My hormones are beginning to rage and froth. Even just looking at her gets them going. Now I know how Bones felt when he grabbed Nasreen Flynn and pressed his lips against hers. I have made up my mind: by the time I reach Z, I am going to have pressed my lips against Lucy's!

I just wish I knew how to begin. I can't do what Bonesy did as we are never on our own together, and even if we were I am not sure I would dare. Maybe this is because my hormones are not yet raging enough. Maybe if I keep gazing at Lucy they'll do a sudden splurge and I'll be like a ravening beast and jump on her!

I have been made a library assistant. This is great as it means that on two days a week you get to stay in the library during your dinner break instead of having to go out and brave the elements (by which I mean Kelvin Clegg and his gang) along with all the rest. You wear a special badge saying LIBRARY ASSISTANT and you stamp the books when they go out and remove the tickets when they come back in. You can also, if you're not too busy, sit down and have a read.

Last term it was one of my greatest ambitions to be made a library assistant, and now it has happened. If Lucy could have been made one with me, I would have been in heaven, but it was not to be. (Mainly because I don't think Lucy reads books.) The other one from my year is Harmony Hynde. I have nothing against Harmony Hynde, except that I don't think she will do much for my hormones. She is not the sort of girl to make your hormones rage. I don't mean to be sexist, but some girls do and some girls don't and that is just a fact of life.

When I got home wearing my badge, my sister was there. She said, "Only nerds get to be made library assistants."

I have been pondering this. Am I a nerd? I may have been last term. I may have been on Monday. But on Tuesday I fell in love with Lucy and my hormones started up. I lust after Lucy! It makes me feel quite macho.

But I think Harmony Hynde may be one. A nerd, I mean. Not just because she is a library assistant but because of everything about her. She is just a very nerdy sort of person. I realise, of course, that she can't help it. It's hardly her fault she has to wear glasses and have a brace on her teeth. It's simply a cruel trick of nature.

Like her hair. Lucy's hair is smooth and silky, the colour of spun gold. Harmony's is a mad messy frizz like a Brillo pad, the colour of carrots.

You can't expect all girls to have hair like Lucy's.

In English, Mr Mounsey told us to think of figures of speech for Monday's lesson. This evening Dad arrived home and announced that it was raining cats and dogs. I said, "Is that a figure of speech?" Dad said, "No, it's a damned nuisance."

But I think it is a figure of speech. It's going to be my one for Monday!

C is for chuck
As in chuck up, or spew.
As in, "I'm going to chuck up
All over you."

I only wrote that because my sister said to me this morning, "Throw *up*!"

I don't know why she said it. I don't know why she says a lot of the things that she says. She is a total mystery.

I realise too late that C could also be for cup sizes… I have learnt all about them! Stuart Sprague told us. Me and Bonesy. He did these drawings to illustrate. A is small,

B is medium, C is large,

D is huge and E is simply humungous!

Bonesy asked Stoo how he knew all of this, and Stoo tapped the side of his nose and closed one eye and said, "I know a whole lot of things. Specially about women... anything you want to know about women, you come to me!"

It is interesting, how people are gifted in different ways. Bones, for instance, is brilliant at woodwork, metalwork, anything to do with making things. I am quite good at exams and stuff. But we are both dead ignorant when it comes to women. Even Bones, in spite of having pressed flesh with Nasreen Flynn. (Which actually was almost a year ago. He's never done it since and he certainly didn't know about cup sizes.) Stuart Sprague is Special Needs but he has this incredible wealth of erudition – meaning *learning* – that me and Bones have entirely missed out on. It really makes you think.

Now that I have been let into the mysteries of cup sizes I am finding it very difficult to stop myself staring at breasts and wondering what size they are. I wonder what size Lucy is? Maybe only an A at the moment, as she is not yet fully grown. But once she is... whew! I reckon it'll be about a G or an H!

Do they make them that big???

The mind boggles!

On Monday we did figures of speech. I told Mr Mounsey my one, raining cats and dogs, and he said it was an excellent choice and did anyone happen to know the name for this particular type of phrase? At which old Harmony shoots her hand up and goes,

"It's a cliché!"

Mr Mounsey said "Well, yes that is certainly one name for it – cliché. Meaning worn out or hackneyed."

I looked at Harmony with some annoyance. What a nerd!

Mr Mounsey then went on to tell us that as well as being a cliché, my figure of speech was also a *metaphor*.

"This is when one thing – the rain – is said to actually be another thing – cats and dogs."

Kelvin Clegg immediately shouted out, "How can rain be cats and dogs?"

Kelvin Clegg is lower down the scale of evolution than an amoeba, but I think he actually had a point there. How can rain be cats and dogs?

You could tell that Mr Mounsey was at a bit of a loss. He went on about symbolism in a very vague sort of way. Just burbling, really. Obviously didn't have the faintest idea. He was saved by the bell, as teachers often are. He said, "Yes, well! Why don't you all go away and try thinking of other figures of speech that are metaphors?"

I have been trying to think of one but it is not easy at the moment as my mind is on other things. Well, when I say other things... what I mean is *sex*. What

I mean is *kissing*. What I mean is... *Lucy*!

My hormones are positively seething.

I asked Dad last night when he started going with girls. He said, "So long ago I can't even remember."

I urged him to try. I know he is getting on and his memory may be going, but this sort of knowledge is very important to me. It is a vital part of my education.

"When did you first kiss a girl?"

"Oh, I can remember that!" chuckled Dad. "That was Jenny Libovitch. We were six years old."

Blimey! I am definitely a late developer. I have a lot of catching up to do!

D is for diarrhoea
Also known as THE RUNS.
It comes from fear
Or from upset tums.
It is gross and mucky.
Decidedly yucky.

And I wish my sister could get it! I wish she would break out into a hideous rash and all her toenails drop off and her hair fall out in great chunks. While we were eating tea, the phone rang and she rushed off to get it. Whenever the phone rings in this house it is almost always for her. She leads this mad social life full of hectic activity. I don't know how she gets to have so many friends as she is a really quite obnoxious person.

She came back into the kitchen chanting, "Sally's got a girlfriend, Sally's got a girlfriend!"

I fixed her with this stony look. (This is something I have been practising.) I said, "What are you talking about?"

She said, "Your girlyfriend! She's on the phone."

I said, "I haven't got a girlyfriend."

"Well, whoever it is," said Izzy, "it's a female person and it's waiting for you."

My heart did this battering thing that hearts do when you are agitated. Or maybe it was my hormones starting up. The only girl I could think of was – Lucy!

It wasn't Lucy, however, it was Harmony Hynde. Ringing to tell me about cats and dogs. She said, "I suddenly remembered! We've got this book at home called Brewer's Dictionary of Phrase & Fable, so I looked it up. Raining cats and dogs... it's really interesting! Do you want to hear?"

I did, sort of, so I said all right, and she said, "I'll read it to you. Listen! In Northern mythology – "

It might have been quite instructive if I'd been able to pay attention properly, but my hormones were raging like mad and all I could think was why couldn't it have been Lucy? Well, and I also found myself wondering what cup size Harmony Hynde was and deciding that she probably wasn't any cup size at all. I mean, that girl is totally flat. She is like a playing card.

It's very bad for the concentration when all you can think of is cup sizes. So the only bit I really got was the last bit, how the cat can be taken as a symbol of pouring rain and the dog as a symbol of strong gusts of wind.

"My dog is certainly a symbol of that," said Harmony.

I held the phone away from my ear and stared at it. Did she mean what I thought she meant?

"He farts," said Harmony; and she made this loud trumpeting noise down the phone and laughed this shrill laugh. "My dad says he's like a wind machine!"

I was a bit gobsmacked, actually. It's quite embarrassing when a girl uses a word like that. It's not what you expect. I mean, I know my sister uses words like that. She uses them all the time. But my sister's a very crude person. Mum's always telling her to wash her mouth out. I wouldn't expect that sort of language from someone that's a library assistant. Specially not Harmony Hynde.

"Where did you get my number from, anyway?" I said, sternly.

Harmony laughed her raucous laugh – she has this really loud, pealing sort of laugh – and told me that I wasn't exactly hard to find.

"There's only one d'Amato in the book!"

I hadn't thought of that. I would have done, if she hadn't gone and confused me. It's just my brain wasn't functioning properly. I found this distinctly annoying. So I grunted in a Neanderthal way and told her that as a matter of fact I was in the middle of my tea, and I think the message must have got through as she was off the phone *pronto* (as my dad would say).

When I went back to the kitchen Mum was all agog (or is it just gog? It is a very strange word) wanting to know who had rung me. Mum is full of insatiable curiosity. I said, "It was a library assistant explaining my metaphor."

There was a silence. Mum blinked, Dad shot me a glance over his glasses. He's probably never heard of metaphors. I don't imagine you'd need them, for being a dentist. Then my sister gave this mad cackle and said, "So that's what you get up to in the library! I might have known it was something disgusting!"

Are all girls like this? Rude and foul-mouthed? It is a sobering thought. It shows once again how little I know about them.

Anyway. That was yesterday. Today is Saturday and I went swimming in the morning with Bones. All night long – well, for quite a large part of it – I lay awake having this fantasy of Lucy being there, in a bikini, and of me having to dive in and rescue her from drowning. Instead of which, guess what? Harmony Hynde comes prancing up (in a one-piece bathing suit that makes her look scrawnier than ever. No cup size at all).

"Salvatore!" she goes.

At least she doesn't call me Sal. I suppose that is a point in her favour. But I do hope she is not going to start dogging my footsteps! I mean, what was she doing at the baths? She's never been there before.

"Do you come here often?" she trills.

"Every Saturday," says Bones, before I can stop him.

What a thicko!

"I've only just started," gushes Harmony. "It's nice, isn't it?"

Fortunately she can't swim very well so we were able to junk her. We left her messing about in the shallow end. Even then she grabbed us on the way out. She seemed to want to be friendly, but I swiftly discouraged it. I explained that me and Bones had things to do.

As we walked away Bones said, "What's the matter? Don't you like her?"

It's not that I don't like her. It's that she doesn't do anything for my hormones, and they have to be my priority if I am ever going to catch up with Dad.

It's nine o'clock now and my sister has gone to a party. Well, she says it's a rave but I don't really see how you can rave on Coca Cola, which is all she's allowed to drink. She went off looking like a Christmas tree, all hung about with bits and pieces. She's always going to parties. I can't understand how she gets all these

34

invitations. People surely can't *like* her? She is quite reasonable-looking, I suppose, but Mum's Match friend didn't say anything about her being a charmer. Well, you hardly could, the way she carries on. She has this extremely vicious temper. She threatened to gouge my eyes out the other day all because she caught me eyeing her bra on the washing line. I was only trying to find out what cup size she was! About A minus, I should think. A at the most. But I didn't get a chance to look properly.

It is a mystery to me how some people have a social life and others don't. I don't have any at all. I just sit in my room dreaming of Lucy. I think I shall resume work on my novel. I have decided what it is going to be about. It is about a cockroach – a low, unlovely form of life, shunned by all and sundry. This is how it is going to start:

I am a cockroach.

Mr Mounsey told us in English that it is very important to have a good snappy start to a book. I think that is definitely snappy.

I should think anyone would want to read a book that started like that.

I have thought of another figure of speech: it's coming down in buckets.

E, is for eyeful
When Lucy walks by.
"Get a load of that!"
The lads all cry.

I have become a sex fiend! My mind is like a sewer. I cannot stop thinking about boobs and bras and cup sizes.

I have got to kiss someone soon!

I have got to kiss Lucy...

I am practising, for when she lets me. I have discovered that if you make a fist and kiss the finger and thumb bit, it feels like lips. Well, sort of. I mean, you have to use your imagination. But I feel it is essential to get some experience before I do it with Lucy. Stuart Sprague says it is very easy to miss, especially if you close your eyes, which he says a lot of people automatically do.

Then instead of pressing lips to lips you find you're pressing lips to eyebrows or lips to nose. So now, every night, I am making a fist and pretending it is Lucy. I am even doing the tongue bit! Though Stuart Sprague says that this is a very advanced form of kissing and should not be attempted on your first go.

"Best get to know 'em," he says, "before you try that."

I think probably Stuart knows what he is talking about. He has kissed more than twenty girls!!!

Bones wanted me to ask him what a bosom felt like, so I did, but he rolled his eyes and said, "Man, I can't tell you! I don't have the words. A bosom has to be experienced to be believed."

I would like to experience a bosom. I think I am becoming *obsessed*.

Today on the way home I had this mad urge to climb up the statue of Queen Victoria in the High Street and touch her tits. This is scary!

Suppose I go mad and lose control of myself? I could be locked up!

On Tuesday, in PSE, we did role playing. Mothers and fathers! Kelvin Clegg had to be sent out. I really hoped I'd get Lucy for a partner, but Carrie Pringle grabbed me, instead. She got in just ahead of Harmony Hynde, who I could see was making for me.

My first thought was that if I couldn't have Lucy I'd sooner have Carrie than be stuck with Harmony, who is acting rather too bold for my liking. But now I am not so sure. Carrie is almost as bad-tempered as my sister. I think she may be a man-hater. Bones said, "She's scary, that one!"

Bones is right. She's a terrible person! Mrs Petty gave all the boys a bean bag to hold. A bean bag with a nappy. She said, "This is your new-born baby. I want you to look after it."

Kelvin Clegg immediately chucked his baby at the wall bars (we were doing it in the gym). That was when he was sent out. I think he was under the impression he was being funny, but lots of the girls sucked their breath in and old Carrie, she makes this angry hissing noise in my ear. Harmony says, "He could get life for that," and Carrie goes, "Yeah! Dead right!"

Mrs Petty said that we would address the issue of male violence another day, and told us to get on with looking after our offspring.

Carrie started in on me straight away.

"You idiot! Don't hold it like that! It's a baby, not a bean bag... well, support its head, for goodness' sake! A new-born baby can't be expected to support itself, can it? Don't you know anything? You'd better watch me making a bottle for it. Are you watching? There, I've made it. Now I'm going to give it to you to give to the baby. Well, go on! Give it to him! Now you can burp him. I said, *burp* him! Don't you even know how to burp him? Honestly, you're pathetic! Give him back and I'll show you... there! He's done it. Now I'm going to go shopping and leave you alone with him. This is a test, to see if you can manage."

When she got back from shopping she claimed she could hear the baby crying. She said, "Are you deaf, or what? Poor little thing! It needs its nappy changed."

I said, "How do you know?"

"Because I can smell it!" she snapped.

While I was changing the bean bag's nappy, Mrs Petty came over. She nodded approvingly and said, "Well done, Salvatore!" But Carrie huffed and puffed and said, "Some father you'd make! Don't know the first thing!"

Actually, I think I did quite well. Bones dropped his one, and Stuart Sprague put his one on the floor and then went and trod on it. I said, "Squashed baby!" Carrie didn't even smile. She said, "*Men!*"

I'm really glad it's Lucy that I fancy and not Carrie. Bones reckons she's a Lesbian.

F is for flob
Meaning cob from the gob.
It's also for fart
Called by Cockneys jam tart.

This is a rather childish sort of rhyme but I think I have to be allowed to express the carefree side of my nature now and again. My life has suddenly become deadly serious. My whole future is at stake. I'm not joking! If my love life is not sorted by the time I reach Z, I shall know for sure there is something wrong with me.

Today is Saturday. An important day in the letters of my alphabet. I went out with Lucy!!! Well, when I say out... it wasn't a date, exactly. What happened was, I sort of bumped into her, accidentally by chance, in the shopping centre. Well, when I say chance... it wasn't entirely chance. I have to be honest. I knew she was going to be there. I heard her talking to

Sharleen Oates in the bus queue on Friday.

Sharleen Oates is her best friend. They were making plans for Saturday. I heard Lucy say, "OK, I'll wait by the Swiss clock." Then Sharleen said, "Wait till eleven. If I'm not there by then, you'll know we didn't get back in time."

Back from where? Who cares! This was my Big Chance. I knew I had to take it. So I told Bones I couldn't go swimming and rushed off to the shopping centre, where I secreted myself in a doorway and watched.

Well! It finally got to be eleven and old Sharleen still hadn't shown, so just as Lucy was starting to move away I sprang out and said, "Hi!"

She jumped about two metres. She said, "Oh. It's you." She didn't sound all that pleased to see me, but probably she thought I was a mugger, or something.

I couldn't think what to say after I'd said hi. Lucy said, "Have you been spying on me?"

I said, "No. I only just got here." (You can't always tell them the exact truth. Stuart Sprague advised me about this.) I said that maybe she'd like me to walk with her, wherever she was going. I said, "I don't think it's safe, being on your own."

Lucy said, "Why not? What's going to happen?"

I said, "There might be men waiting to abduct you."

"Oh, yeah?" she said. "And what use d'you think you'd be?"

I said, "Well, I could stop them!"

"You and whose army?" she said.

She's very quick at that sort of thing. Wit and repartee. I find it quite difficult to keep up with her.

In the end she said that if I wanted I could buy her a Coke. So that is what I did. The first time I have ever bought a Coke for a girl! We sat together in the Swiss Snack Bar and my hormones roared and bubbled and I wanted to grab her and press my lips against hers, only I didn't think she'd go for it. Not in the Swiss Snack Bar. Not in front of people.

After we'd drunk our Cokes I asked her if she'd like to come for a walk. She said, "What for?" I said, "We could go to the park. It's nice in the park." She said, "No, it's not, it's freezing cold." "I could always hold your hand," I said.

I obviously moved a bit too fast. She looked at me like I'd made some kind of improper suggestion. Like instead of saying "I could always hold your hand," I'd said "I could always hold your bosom."

Suppose I really did say that? Suppose that's what

I said and I didn't realise it? I'm losing control! I have bosoms on the brain! I'm in sexual overdrive!

I am going to write some more of my novel, *I Am A Cockroach.*

I find that the life of a cockroach, although inevitably a sad one, has a calming effect on the hormones. Cockroaches do not have bosoms.

I have just had to break off and go downstairs. Mum called to me that I was wanted on the phone. I can hardly believe it! It was Harmony Hynde. *Again!* She wanted to know why I wasn't at the baths this morning. Cheek! What's it to her?

She said she's found another figure of speech for me: Going at it hammer and tongs.

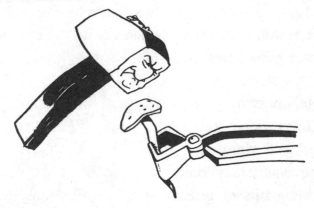

It is quite a good one. But I think Harmony Hynde must have even less social life than me.

G is for grolly
Which comes out the nose.
A really good grolly
Hangs down to your toes.

My sister says I'm a pervert. All because she caught me fingering – that's what she called it: *fingering* – her bra. It was there again, on the line! I just wanted to know what it felt like. She didn't have to go running off and tell Mum.

"Mum, he's a pervert! He's got to be stopped!"

Mum said, "Salvatore, whatever it is you're doing to upset your sister, just stop it."

"He's perving!" cried Iz.

"Don't perve on your sister," said Mum.

She was pretty busy, shredding bits of grass. Well, that's what it looked like. (It's what it tasted like, too.)

"He's a lunatic! He ought to be locked up!" screeched Iz.

Mum sighed and said, "Can't you two just manage to co-exist like a normal brother and sister?"

"We could if one of us wasn't seriously *ab*normal!" snapped Izzy. "Revolting little freak!"

I feel very misunderstood, though I suppose I shouldn't complain. Some of the greatest names of history have been sneered at and vilified. Not that I can actually think of any offhand, but I know it to be true. It is what is happening in my life at this very moment.

Yesterday, for instance, at school, Sharleen Oates accused me of looking up her skirt. But I wasn't! Well, not on purpose. I didn't mean to look up it. She ought to wear skirts that are a bit longer if she doesn't want people looking up them. Hers hardly even covers her bum.

"You were looking at my knickers!" she screeched.

Girls always screech when they get mad. This is something I have noticed. They screech very loudly and hurt your ears. It is like a kind of weapon.

What made her think I'd want to look at her knickers, anyway? They were pink, as a matter of fact. She had holes in her tights where the pinkness poked through. This is so disgusting! I hope Lucy doesn't have holes in her tights.

Old Sharleen, she didn't half carry on! She's got this really high-pitched squawk and her eyes bulge out.

"I suppose you enjoyed that, didn't you? I suppose you get a kick out of looking up girls' skirts? Looking at their knickers!"

Lucy said, "You want to watch that one! He's trouble."

And then she gave me another of her looks and went flouncing off up the stairs, dragging Sharleen with her. Bones said to me later, "She fancies you!" I asked him how he knew, and he said, "It's the way they behave when they fancy you."

"How do you mean?" I said.

"Well," said Bones. And he waved a hand. "Slagging you off. Making like they think you're dirt, while all the time they're secretly lusting after you."

I would like to believe him, but I am not sure how reliable Bones is. And in any case, what about Sharleen Oates? She was slagging me off like crazy. So was Carrie Pringle, if it comes to that. Don't say they both lust after me!!! I couldn't take it!!! If I'm not careful I shall have a whole line of girls queueing up for my body.

But I shall always remain faithful to Lucy. She is my first and only love. The others are as dust beneath her chariot wheels. They can grovel as much as they like. Lucy is the one for me!

I have written a poem for her. I did it this evening when I was supposed to be doing my maths homework. This is my poem.

Poem for Lucy

Lovely, lovable, luscious Lucy,
Charming, cherry-lipped, cherubic and juicy!
Sublime, superb and sparkling Luce,
So dainty and dazzling, even in puce!

Sweet as sugar, sweet as a nut,
Sweet as honey, there's no but.
Sweet to the senses, sweet to the ear,
Your voice is a delight to hear!

Exquisite, enchanting one,
Like a glowing, golden sun!
Shine on me, o bright-eyed being!
Do not send your suitor fleeing.

Thou radiant maid of the rosy cheek,
Accept the love of one so meek.

I am quite excited. I think I might have written a sonnet! I am going to give it to Lucy at school tomorrow. She will be unable to resist!

In the meantime, I am being stalked by Harmony Hynde. I have heard of *men* being stalkers. I didn't 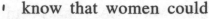 know that women could do it. She is stalking me everywhere I go! She hangs around at the end of class. She jumps out of cupboards. (She jumped out of the stationery cupboard and nearly gave me a heart attack.) She *looms* at  the foot of staircases. Today she waited for me so that we could go to the library together. Kelvin Clegg was there. He shouted, "Whey-hey! Fun and games behind the bike shed!"

Harmony said, "Don't mind him. He's just a bonehead."

I know that she is right and that Kelvin Clegg's

mental ability is about zero to the power of nothing, and that anyone with even the grain of a brain ought to be able to rise above it. But it irritates the hell out of me! I mean this most sincerely.

I did my best to shake Harmony off. I said, "Oh! I've suddenly remembered."

"What?" she said.

"Something I've forgotten!"

I dived back into the classroom, but she dived back with me so fast we nearly got jammed together in the doorway. Kelvin Clegg gave this really lewd sort of laugh and went loping off down the corridor making obscene gestures and going, "Sally Tomato! Whey-hey-hey!"

Now he'll tell everyone that I fancy Harmony Hynde. She has no right to do this to me! I could probably get her stopped by law. I could put the police on to her. Girls shouldn't be allowed to make boys' lives a misery this way.

H is for halitosis
Meaning, oh boy! What a pong!
When you breathe upon someone,
As in speech, or in song,
And they take great offence
At the horrible stench,
Reeling backwards with howls
And ear-splitting yowls
"I'm not feeling well!
I can't stand the smell!"

Let the moral of this story be:
Brush your teeth reg-u-lar-ly.
(I put this bit in for Dad.)

It is very difficult to tell if you have halitosis. I am
worried that I might have. I have tried cupping my
hands over my face and breathing into them but the
smell seems to evaporate before you can get a whiff
of it.

Of course, there may not be any smell. I just wish

I could be sure! How can I kiss Lucy if I am worried about stinking her out with drains and bad eggs???

I breathed a few times over my sister tonight, just to see if she would reel backwards, but she stuck her elbow in my stomach and yelled at Mum.

"Mum, he's doing it again!"

"Doing what?" said Mum.

"Behaving like a pervert!"

"Salvatore, whatever it is that you're doing, stop it," said Mum. She was mixing up a mess to stuff something with. (Stuffed onions. Yuck!)

"But he's breathing on me!" wailed Iz.

"So what?" I said. "I can't very well stop breathing, can I?"

"You don't have to do it over me! God, you're such a pervert!"

She didn't say, "God, you stink." Which is what she probably would have done if I did. So I think I probably don't. But I'd still like to be sure!

Your first kiss is something that shapes the rest of your life. Bones has told me this. He says he will never forget kissing Nasreen Flynn.

"It's made me the man I am today. Know what I mean?"

He doesn't count his cousin, as she took him by surprise.

"Wasn't really what I'd call an experience. She jumped on me. I didn't have a chance to respond."

It's very important that it should be an experience. If it doesn't work, Bones reckons, it can cast a blight on your entire existence. He reckons it's responsible for a lot of the crimes in this country. Men whose first kiss has been a disaster.

"I reckon it's something you never get over."

This is why I'm so worried about having halitosis!

I have just climbed into bed and pulled the duvet over my head and breathed in and out really deeply. It got a bit fuggy in there but there wasn't any smell. Maybe I am agonising over nothing.

Today I gave Lucy my poem that I wrote for her. I put it in an envelope and wrote *For Lucy* on the front in curly writing. She said, "What's this?" I said, "It's for you." She said, "I can see that! What is it?"

"Something I've written," I said. "But you're not to read it until you're on your own."

I didn't want her showing it to Sharleen Oates.

Lucy said, "It's not anything rude, is it?"

I said, "No! It's nice. But I want you to be on your own so that you can really appreciate it."

Needless to say, old Sharleen was there, glued to her side as usual. She gave this inane cackle and went, "He thinks you're going to eat it!"

Lucy tossed her head. "It had better not be anything rude," she said.

It's terrible, the way they don't trust you. I hope she hasn't had bad experiences.

Later, when school got out, I bumped into her at the bus stop. On her own! I said, "Where's Sharleen?" She said, "What's it to you?" Which immediately got me tongue-tied. She's very sharp, is Lucy. Very on the ball. She mightn't do too well in tests and suchlike, but she's extremely quick-witted.

"I hope you don't think you're going to start grabbing me," she said, "just because I'm by myself."

She must have had bad experiences. Otherwise, why would she think such a thing? I just want to kiss her!

All the same, I felt a bit emboldened as I don't think she'd have said it unless secretly, inside herself, she quite liked the idea. (I think at last I am beginning to understand girls a bit better!) I said, "How about meeting up in the shopping centre, Saturday?"

"What for?" she said.

I said, "I dunno! Just thought it might be fun."

"Why?" she said. "What'd we do?"

"Walk about," I said. "Look at things."

"What things?"

I said, "Anything you like."

"Clothes? Make-up?"

"Anything," I said.

"Mmm..." She put her head on one side. "I'm thinking about it," she said.

It kills me when she puts her head on one side like that! Her hair all swings out, like a curtain.

"See you there at 10.30?" I said. "Same place as last time?"

She said, "I haven't decided yet."

"You could look at all the clothes you wanted," I said.

"Mmm..." She tilted her head the other way.

"So d'you fancy the idea?" I said.

"Might do," she said. "Might not. See how I feel."

"I'll be there anyway," I said.

"Suit yourself," said Lucy.

I think this is what is known as teasing. It's what girls do. It's a sign they like you! She really wants to come out with me but doesn't want to seem too keen.

I wish I had some decent clothes to wear. I wish I had some gel to put on my hair. I wonder if my sister's got any? She'd never let me borrow it even if she had. She's dead mean, and anyway she thinks I'm a pervert.

I've just seriously studied myself in the mirror. I think I can understand what Mum's Match friend meant about filling out. I haven't got any muscles! I haven't got any pecs or lats! If I had some weights, I could do some body building.

Question: if I started body building now, right this minute, could I get some muscles going between now and Saturday?

Answer: almost certainly not. Two days isn't anywhere near long enough. But I could always get started!

If I had any weights…

There are some bricks in the garden. They're pretty heavy.

Long pause.

I have made myself some weights! It's dead easy. I could patent the idea. I could be a millionaire!

MAKE YOUR OWN WEIGHTS
Ingredients:
Bricks (any number you think you can lift)
One broom handle
Two plastic carrier bags
Length of garden twine

Method:
Put even number of bricks
in each carrier bag
Tie bags tight with garden twine
Attach to broom handle,
one at each end

It's brilliant! I should have thought of it sooner. I could be positively bulging with muscles by now!

I have been pumping iron all evening. I think I'm already beginning to fill out!

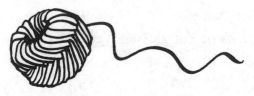

Nearly forgot to say that Harmony Hynde accosted me as I was on my way to PE. Actually she sprang out of the sports cupboard, all toothy and beaming, with her arms full of netballs. She must have been crouched in there, spying through the door crack, waiting for me to come along. She wanted to know if I was going swimming on Saturday. When I said no, she looked really disappointed.

It is so pathetic when women chase men like this! Has she no pride?

She told me she'd thought of another metaphor for my collection. What makes her think I'm collecting them? I asked her what it was, just being polite. I mean, I know she's making my life a misery but she's obviously unbalanced. I wouldn't want to hurt her. She said, "In the teeth of the gale!"

I said, "Is that a metaphor?"

"I think so," she said. "At any rate, it's a figure of speech."

What a sad life that girl must lead.

I is for impure
Thoughts
The sort
Of thoughts
You cannot tell
Your mum about
For fear that she
Would then find out
That her young lad
Is just a lout.

My mind is full of impure thoughts. It is like a sink. Like a sewer. Like a cess pit. I can't seem to stop myself! I am really worried in case I ever have to have an anaesthetic – like for instance if I get a brain tumour. All the contents of my mind would come spewing out!

Spent all yesterday pumping iron ready for meeting Lucy in the shopping centre. Looked in the bathroom cabinet for hair gel but could only find some stuff called Foaming Face Cleanser. It's quite sticky and has a nice smell so I borrowed some and used it on my hair. I thought it worked pretty well, but as I was on my way out my sister caught sight of me. She said, "And what are you today? A lavatory brush?"

She has a really coarse turn of phrase, my sister. I don't know where she gets it from; the rest of us aren't like that.

"What have you done to yourself, anyway?" she says, sounding all suspicious. She leans forward and sniffs at my hair. "That's my face cleanser!" she shrieks. "You stinking little pervert!" Then she gallops upstairs going, "Mum, Mum, he's stolen my face cleanser!"

I got out, pronto.

I had to wait ages before Lucy turned up. While I was waiting, Harmony Hynde came past.

"I've come to buy a new swim suit," she said.

That's what she *said*. I'm not altogether sure that I believe it. I think she was stalking me.

Anyway, we talked for a bit and then she said, "What about calling someone a stick in the mud?" I said, "Like who, for instance?"

"Like anyone that's dull and boring," she said.

"It's another metaphor," she added. "I found it in Brewer's."

I said, "You must spend your entire life reading that book."

"It's interesting," she said. "You'd be surprised the things you learn."

After she'd gone I almost wished she'd stayed longer. I almost wished I was going swimming. But then I saw Lucy coming towards me and my spirits immediately soared, only not quite as high as they might have done. In fact it would be true to say that they were dashed, almost instantly. She'd only gone and brought Sharleen with her! They were clamped together, as usual, arm in arm, marching in step.

"Well, look who it isn't!" said Sharleen.

"Been here long?" said Lucy.

I told her that I'd been there for almost half an hour. I said, "I thought we were going to meet at 10.30?"

"I said I might," said Lucy.

"She said she might," said Sharleen.

And then for absolutely no reason at all they started to giggle.

Girls are always giggling. It's very offputting, especially when you don't know what they're giggling about.

"Oh, look!" chirruped Sharleen. "He's put egg white on his hair!"

I said, "It's not egg white, it's foaming gel."

"How sweet!" said Lucy. "All right, Sally Tomato! You can come with us if you want. He'll be useful for carrying stuff," she said to Sharleen.

"And for buying Cokes," said Sharleen. And then they giggled. *Again*.

Girls are seriously weird. When me and Bones go to the shopping centre we like to visit Model World, or if we have any money we go to the video games arcade. If we don't have any money we ask people if we can take their shopping trolleys back for them and keep the pound coins. Other times we just hang around in the car park on our roller blades and set car alarms off. We play this game.

"The red Merc... I dare you!"

"Jag in the corner... I dare you!"

Lucy and Sharleen didn't want to do any of these things. All they wanted to do was just trail round the shops looking at clothes and make-up and stuff. When we'd finished doing that they said I could buy them a Coke, and when they'd drunk their Cokes Lucy said, "Well, I reckon that's it, then," and they both got up and walked off.

I ran after them and said, "Where are you going?"

"Home," said Sharleen. "Not that it's any business of yours."

She's very aggressive. Bones would say it's because she fancies me.

I said, "Shall I come to the bus stop with you?"

Lucy said, "Can if you like."

When we got to the bus stop, I said, "Shall I walk you home?"

"Up to you," said Lucy.

"What's he want to walk us home for?" said Sharleen.

Lucy said, "Stop us being abducted."

"This is it," I said. "You can't be too careful."

Specially Lucy. I don't know as anyone'd want to abduct Sharleen.

Lucy got off the bus first. I got off with her. Sharleen stuck her head out of the window and shrieked, "I s'pose you don't care about me being abducted!"

"Well?" said Lucy. "*Do* you?"

I assured her that I did. I mean, Sharleen being her friend and all.

Lucy said, "Do you care about her being abducted as much as you care about me being abducted?"

I said, "No! Didn't you read my poem that I wrote for you?"

Lucy said, "Yeah!" and giggled.

"It wasn't meant to be funny," I said. "I really meant it."

"It's love poetry," said Lucy. "Soppy love poetry! The sort of stuff them old guys did."

I said, "What old guys?"

"Them old guys… Shakespeare, and that."

We did a Shakespeare sonnet in English a few weeks ago. *Shall I Compare Thee to a Summer's Day?* (To which Kelvin Clegg yelled "Back end of a cow, more like!" and got sent out.) I didn't know that Lucy had even been listening. I'd thought she was asleep.

It's quite flattering, being compared with Shakespeare.

"Would you like me to write another one?" I said. "I'll write you another one!"

"Can't wait," said Lucy.

Hooray! Lucy likes my poetry! It's Valentine's Day next week. I shall compose a Valentine for her.

I have been pumping iron like crazy. I think I might have a muscle coming.

J is for Jimmy
Whose surname is Riddle.
To go for a Jimmy
Means go for a piddle.

I told this to Bones, who thought it was extremely amusing. I wouldn't dare tell it to Lucy! I don't think girls would find it funny.

I asked Bones if he ever had impure thoughts. He said, "What kind of impure thoughts?" I said, "About girls." He thought about it and said, "What would count as impure?" I said, "Boobs?" Bones admitted that he thought quite a lot of thoughts about boobs.

"Do you reckon girls think about us the way we think about them?" I said.

Bones said he didn't know. I don't, either. I wish that I did!

I have written my Valentine for Lucy.

Valentine for Lucy

Love is blind
You must be, too,
If you don't know
How I feel about you.
So please will you be
My Valentine?
I'll be yours
If you'll be mine!

I have put my phone number, very small, at the bottom. She won't know who it's from, but she might ring up to find out! I'm going to send it first class, so that she will get it on The Day.

I have written URGENT!!! PLEASE DELIVER WITHOUT DELAY!!! This is to make sure the postman doesn't think, Oh, this is not very important, I will put it back in the box.

They do this sometimes. Well, according to Dad they do. Mum says Dad is paranoid. This means thinking that people are out to get you. I feel like this with Harmony Hynde when she stalks me.

It is now half term. The week stretches before me, Lucyless and empty. I can't even pump iron. Yesterday evening, in the middle of pumping, a disaster occurred. One of the bags of bricks flew off the end of the broom handle and crashed into the wall, knocking a great chunk out of it.

Mum immediately came flying upstairs going, "What was that? What's happened? What have you done?" Then my sister appeared and gave this futile screech of laughter.

"Hey! Wow! Get a load of that! Mr Universe in person!"

I don't think it's right she should come bursting in when I am clad only in my pants. It is not decent.

Mum said, "Why are you throwing bags of bricks around your bedroom?"

I said, "I'm practising."

"For what?" said Mum.

I said, "For Sports Day… for the brick-throwing contest."

"Do you also have a broom handle contest?" said Mum.

"Oh! That," I said. And I gave this little laugh. "We put bricks on the end and we hurl them."

"Well, we do not hurl them in our bedroom," said Mum. "Your father is going to be very displeased with you."

So now I don't have my weights any more. And I was definitely getting a muscle! Two muscles. One in each of my arms.

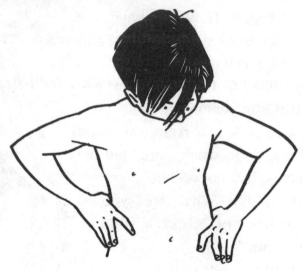

I have made a resolution. I am going to devote the whole of half term to building myself up. Just because I can no longer pump iron doesn't mean I should be idle. I intend to do twenty press-ups a day and swim twenty lengths of the pool.

I am also going to write some more of *I Am A*

Cockroach. I feel strangely sympathetic towards cockroaches. They are harmless, even pleasant creatures when you get to know them, yet people treat them with the deepest loathing and contempt. It is the way my sister treats me. She goes on about how I am a pervert, then comes bursting into my bedroom when I am wearing nothing but my pants. It is not right. It should not be allowed. She is the pervert, if anyone is.

I have thought of another saying: he's got eyes in the back of his head.

I must tell this to Harmony when I see her. She can look it up in her Brewer's book.

K is for knockers and knickers
and kiss.
The first two are rude, but the
third one is bliss!

Today I did twenty press-ups and swam twenty
lengths of the pool. Bones couldn't come as he has
gone to visit his gran, but Stuart Sprague was there
and we went upstairs to have a Coke. I told Stoo my
poem about knockers and knickers, and he said,
"Kissing can be bliss. But you've got to get the right
lips."

He is an expert on lips! He told me how there are
many different kinds. Thin ones, thick ones, big
ones, small ones, soft ones, hard ones, mean, tight
prune-like ones, lips that wriggle like worms, lips
that turn in on themselves, lips that are smooth, lips
that are scaley, lips that are warm and velvety, lips
that are luscious.

"You get all types," said Stuart.

I thought of Lucy's lips. Will I ever get to kiss them???

"That was a good poem, that was," said Stuart. "I'll remember that one better 'n all that stuff we do at school."

"I've got another one you might like," I said. "I'm writing one for every letter of the alphabet."

I told him about F is for flob. He liked that one. I found this very encouraging and was just about to tell him J is for Jimmy when Harmony Hynde loomed on the horizon. She made a beeline for us.

"Hi, guys! Can I sit with you?" she said.

Stuart said, "Yeah! Sal was just telling me this poem he's written."

I frowned at him, warningly, but old Stoo isn't the brightest.

"Go on!" he said. "J is for Jimmy – "

"This sounds good!" said Harmony.

"It's just a bit of nonsense," I muttered.

She said, "I like bits of nonsense!"

"He told us a really good one just now," said Stuart. "Tell her the one you told us just now!"

"Please," begged Harmony.

I said, "I can't. It was rude."

Harmony did this great cackling laugh that she does. "I love things that are rude!"

"Yeah," I said, "but it was very rude."

"No, it wasn't," said Stuart. "Farting ain't all that rude."

"Farting!" cried Harmony, delighted. "Oh, please! I want to hear it!"

So in the end I told it to her. I told her F is for flob and J is for Jimmy, and she shrieked.

"He's got loads more," said Stuart. "He's got one for every letter of the alphabet."

"I will have," I said, "when I've finished."

"Brilliant!" breathed Harmony. "Disgusting Ditties!"

I think perhaps I may have gone a bit red. I do have this annoying tendency to blush.

"It's all right," she assured me, "it's quite respectable… if Roald Dahl could have Revolting Rhymes, I don't see why you can't have Disgusting Ditties. You might even be able to get them published!"

I never thought of that. I have considered getting *I Am A Cockroach* published as this is literature and quite classy. But the alphabet – well! As I said modestly to Harmony, the alphabet is just a way of passing an idle moment.

"Better'n that stuff we do at school," said Stuart.

He wanted to hear some more so I told them G is for grolly and C is for chuck, and he and Harmony immediately started pretending to chuck up and pull grollies out of their noses.

"Look at this one!" yelled Stuart, stretching an imaginary grolly down to the ground.

"Watch out, I'm going to throw up!" cried Harmony. *"Blurgh!"*

I am surprised at a girl like Harmony behaving in such a childish fashion. She is supposed to have a brain. She always comes top of everything. I'm sure Lucy wouldn't have laughed. I'm not sure that a girl should.

Tuesday

I have decided I am going to write this every day while we are on half term. It will be good practice.

This morning I did my press ups and went to the pool. Harmony was there. Again! She is definitely stalking me. I suppose I shall just have to accept it.

We went upstairs for a Coke – I mean, I didn't specially want to, but I didn't have anything else to do and you can't just ignore people. I told her about eyes in the back of your head, and she said she would see if it was in Brewer's. Then she told me that she had written a Disgusting Ditty for my collection. She gave me a copy of it. It is quite good.

S is for scab
which perhaps you might get
If you slip when it's wet
And graze a knee
Or slide on a pea
Or even, maybe,
Jab very hard at yourself with a pen
And make a big hole which bleeds and then
If left alone,
Not gnawed like a bone,
Will form a most delightful crust,
The colour of dried blood, or rust,
Which you can pick and even eat.
Scabby sarny! What a treat!

She said, "You can use it, if you want."

She seemed really keen so I said that I would think about it - though as a matter of fact I already have one for S. One that I cannot possibly tell Harmony Hynde about!!! Or anyone else, for that matter. It is too personal.

"It's fun, isn't it?" said Harmony, beaming. "Maybe I'll do an alphabet, too, and we could get them published in a collection... Disgusting Ditties, by Salvatore d'Amato and Harmony Hynde."

I must admit, it is quite tempting. I should like to see my name in print.

Harmony asked me if I was going to be at the pool again tomorrow and if I was would I teach her to dive. I said that I would probably be there but couldn't make any promises. It is important not to commit oneself.

Wednesday

Decided I might just as well go swimming. Tried to teach Harmony to dive but she is not very good at it. She is far better at writing poetry. She gave me a copy of another ditty for our book.

A is for ants
That get in your pants.
They get round your middle
And cause you to wriggle.
They get up your nose
And make you snooze.
But the worst thing to fear
Is ants in your ear.
If they get to your brain
You can't stand the strain.
You DIE, demented!
By ants, tormented.

She apologised for the fact that a) it was rather morbid and b) not very rude. She promised to do a really disgusting one for tomorrow.

She also said that she had looked for eyes in the back of your head in her Brewer's Dictionary, but it wasn't there.

"But do you know what sheep's eyes means? It means *to look sheepishly at a person to whom you feel lovingly inclined.*"

I said, "How would you look sheepishly?"

"Dunno," said Harmony. "Like this?"

"Or like this?" I said.

We sat and made sheep's eyes at each other until I got face ache. I cannot imagine making sheep's eyes at Lucy even though I feel lovingly inclined. I wouldn't want to frighten her.

Today is Valentine's Day and my sister had three Valentines. Who on earth would fancy my sister??? I think they were just joke ones, and she doesn't realise.

Lucy hasn't rung me. Perhaps she's too shy.

Thursday

Harmony is writing ditties like crazy! She's now done ones for B, C and D. B is for bottom, D is for dirt. I won't say what C is for. I think she ought to be ashamed of herself. She says that E is going to be only a little bit disgusting. Just as well! You can be prosecuted for this sort of thing.

Lucy still hasn't rung.

Friday

Still haven't heard from Lucy.

Went swimming again. Harmony can now do five lengths. She wants me to teach her backstroke.

She's written some more poems for our Book of Disgusting Ditties.

She said, "Why don't we do illustrations? Illustrations would go really well!" I said, "Can you draw?" She said, "No, but you can!"

It is true, I am quite good at art. It is one of my best subjects. Art and English; those are what I'm best at. Harmony is also good at English, but with her it is English and Music. She said, "We are creative kind of people."

I never thought of it like that.

She said, "It's why we get on so well."

I never thought of that, either. What does she mean, get on so well??? I hope she is not hinting at anything. I haven't written *her* a love poem! Or a Valentine.

I wonder if Harmony got any Valentines? Perhaps I should have sent her one. Just as a friend. I wouldn't have put my phone number on it, no way! I wouldn't want her jumping to conclusions. But it would have been nice for her, as otherwise I don't imagine, probably, that she would have got any.

I think she is definitely an A. Or A double minus.

I asked her today why she came swimming so often. I mean, I know the real reason. The real reason is because she's stalking me. But I was interested to see what excuse she would come up with.

She obviously has a very fertile imagination. She

said it was because of this terrific fear of drowning that she has.

"I thought I ought to learn how to swim."

I suppose it could be true. I mean, she might have this terrific fear of drowning *and* be stalking me, both at the same time.

I told her my fear of getting a brain tumour.

"Except there isn't very much that I can do about that."

Harmony agreed that there wasn't.

I said, "I also have this fear of heights."

"Maybe you should climb some mountains," said Harmony.

I told her that I couldn't; I'd be too scared. I don't mind admitting this sort of thing to Harmony. I wouldn't to Lucy, obviously. It would be very bad for my image.

Harmony said, "I can understand a fear of heights. Some people come over all funny just standing on a chair. But why are you scared of getting a brain tumour?"

I said, "It's because I read this article once about someone that had one. Why are you scared of drowning?"

Harmony said that she'd read a book about some people in a plane crash. Their plane had gone plummeting into the sea and they had all drowned except for just this one person that was an exceptionally strong swimmer.

I said, "I read this book once about some people in a plane crash, only their plane came down in the Andes and the ones that survived ended up eating the ones that didn't. That's pretty gross," I said, "isn't it?"

"Not if they were going to starve," said Harmony.

"What, eating *people*?" I said.

"Why not?" said Harmony. "We eat animals. We *kill* animals. That's gross," she said, "if anything is."

"But imagine if it was your grandmother," I said.

"Why do people always say grandmother?" said Harmony.

I said, "Do they?"

She said, "Yes, always!"

"Well, all right," I said. "Imagine if it was your mum or dad."

She admitted that that would be different. "I expect you might prefer to starve rather than eat your mum and dad. But if you *did* eat them – well! I wouldn't see anything wrong in it. I mean, not if they were dead. They'd probably *want* you to eat them, if it was the only thing that was going to keep you alive. I mean, it's better than going out and killing something. That's the most gross thing there is!"

I said, "Are you a vegetarian, then?"

"Of course I am," said Harmony. "It's the only civilised thing to be."

We then had this really long, deep, meaningful discussion, as a result of which I am prepared to admit that one day, in the future, I may well give up eating flesh as I could certainly not go out and slit a cow's throat, which is what she challenged me to do. She said, "If you couldn't, then you're being hypocritical!"

She is quite an interesting person. But I don't think her lips would be as luscious as Lucy's! I don't think Harmony's lips would be luscious at all.

L is for lips
So soft and juicy.
I long to kiss
The lips of Lucy!

Thinking of lips made me realise that I had only done one ditty for this week. I have to do two! That is the target I set myself.

Was just about to set off to the pool this morning (it is now Saturday) when my sister yelled at me.

"There's another of your women on the phone!"

It was her, it was she, it was Lucy! She said, "Sally Tomato, you are not supposed to put your phone number on a Valentine card."

I said, "How did you know it was me?"

"I'm not daft," said Lucy.

I said, "Did you get loads?"

"Might have," she said.

I think she must have done. But she knew which one was mine!

"I was just ringing," she said, "to say that if you want, you can meet me in the shopping centre and buy me a Coke."

Bliss bliss bliss! I couldn't believe it... she was asking me to go out with her!

I dumped my swimming things, nicked another blob of my sister's foaming face cleanser and went steaming off to the shopping centre. While I was waiting for Lucy I tried thinking of things that I could talk to her about, so that I wouldn't embarrass myself by having nothing to say. But then the minute she appeared I became, like, totally tongue-tied.

Hey! That's another one. *Tongue-tied.*

We went and I bought us both a Coke and I still couldn't think of anything to say, I mean I just didn't know what to talk to her about. I was starting to get really twitchy in case my mouth suddenly opened of its own accord and said something obscene, like, "What cup size are you?"

I've heard of this sort of thing happening. It's like when you get people walking down the street shouting four-letter words. It's called Tourette's. It's this illness they have where they can't stop swearing. I think as a matter of fact my sister probably suffers from it, yelling words like pervert and other stuff which she could almost certainly get prosecuted for. I am seriously concerned in case it runs in families, which means at any moment I could start doing it myself.

"Don't talk much, do you?" said Lucy.

I said, "I'm the strong and silent type."

"Oh, yeah?" said Lucy. Then she said, "Written any more poetry?"

I was so relieved to have something to talk about that I went and blurted out J is for Jimmy before I could stop myself.

Lucy shrieked, "Sally Tomato, don't be so rude!"

I knew she wouldn't find it funny. I shouldn't have told her. I don't know why I did. It must be my Tourette's starting up.

"Can't you think of anything *not* rude to talk about?" she said.

I said, "I could tell you about this book I read."

"What book?"

"Book where these people were in a plane crash."

"What happened to them?"

"Well, some were killed and some survived, and the ones that survived ended up eating the ones that were killed."

"*Eating* them? That is disgusting!" shrieked Lucy.

"They were dying of starvation," I said.

"That's no excuse! Eating human flesh… ugh!"

"We eat animals," I said.

"That's different," said Lucy.

I said, "Why?"

She said, "Because it is! Don't be stupid."

There wasn't much to talk about after that so I took her back home. But guess what? I almost got to kiss her! My lips touched her cheek… if I had only been a bit bolder I think she might have let me kiss her on the lips. I think she really does like me!

I have spent the afternoon writing a poem to Lucy's cheek.

Poem to Lucy's Cheek

Lucy's cheek, so soft, so squishy,
Unlike some, which are quite fishy.
Lucy's cheek, so soft and dimpled!
Others' cheeks are rough and pimpled.
Not so Lucy's! Lucy's cheek!
The cheek of Luce, a damsel meek,
Is like a golden sun-kissed peach,
Upon a bough just out of reach.
O let me pluck the cheek of Luce!
And deeply drink th'immortal juice.

I can't make up my mind whether to give it to her or not.

When I got home my sister said that my other girlfriend had rung. She said, "How many do you have, you disgusting little pervert? A whole harem?"

I said, "That one is not my girlfriend. She just happens to be in my class."

"Sounded like a girlfriend to me," said Iz. "She was ringing from the swimming pool. Seemed to think you were going to meet her there."

I never said that I would meet her! She might have *thought* that's what I said, but it most certainly was not. All I said was, "See you." See you could mean anything. It could mean, see you tomorrow, or see you next week, or just see you some time. It didn't mean that I was necessarily going to see her *today*. People oughtn't to take things for granted.

I wonder if I should have rung her? She didn't

leave her number. I suppose I could always look it up in the book, but there must be loads of people with the name Hynde. How would I know which one was her?

She should have told Iz her number if she wanted me to ring her.

Tomorrow I will do some pictures to illustrate my poems. I shall take them in to show her and that will make her happy.

Tonight Mum said about someone, "She's like a dog with two tails."

M is for match –
Your cheek, my bum.
This was a joke
When I was young!

I recited this little ditty to Harmony in the library, Monday lunch time. Well, first off I said that I was sorry I wasn't at the pool on Saturday. I said, "I didn't realise you were expecting me. And I couldn't ring because I didn't have your number. If I'd have had your number—"

Harmony said, "You don't have to apologise. I quite understand."

I wasn't sure what she meant by this. Did she mean that she understood about me not having her phone number? Or did she mean that she understood about some girls being the sort to set your hormones off and others just being the sort that you have intellectual conversations with?

I felt kind of sorry for her. I suddenly imagined her waiting and waiting and me not turning up. It wasn't my fault; but I didn't like to see her looking all miserable.

Also I felt that perhaps I had been unnecessarily harsh. I could have looked her up in the telephone directory. I don't expect there are as many Hyndes as all that. So to cheer her up I showed her the pictures I've done for our book. I told her that I would do some to go with her poems, as well, and then I told her the joke about your cheek, my bum. She enjoyed that. She said that she'd got one for me.

"It's another one for the book."

E is elastic that holds up your knicker.
If it should snap, beware!
In the wink of an eye, in a flash, in a flicker,
You'll find that your bottom is bare!

I said, "Hey! That's really good."

I wasn't just saying it. I really meant it! But I don't think she believed me. She got all dejected again and said, "It's only doggerel."

I said, "Yeah, but it's funny."

She said, "Do you really think so?"

"It's ace," I told her. "It'll go great in the book!"

She said, "Mmm... I suppose the third line isn't too bad."

She's very critical of her own work.

Today is Friday and on the way home I bumped into Lucy at the bus stop.

I said, "Where's Sharleen?"

"What's it to you?" she said. "She's at the dentist."

After this interchange, silence descended upon us like a thick cloak. It brought on a touch of the Tourette's. I found myself blurting out my cheek and bum joke. She didn't get it!

I said, "Your cheek, my bum."

She still didn't get it. She said, "Are you being rude again?"

I said, "No. It's a hallowed tradition."

Harmony was the one that told me this.

Lucy said, "A hallo tradition? What are you talking about?"

"It's like those post cards," I said. "Ones you get at the seaside, with fat ladies bursting out of bathing costumes? They're not rude."

"Yes, they are," said Lucy. "They're disgusting!"

"Well, anyway," I said, "Roald Dahl did it."

"Did what?" said Lucy.

"Wrote Revolting Rhymes. There isn't any harm in them."

And for some reason I told her Harmony's one about knicker elastic. I think my Tourette's must be developing really fast.

Lucy said, "Do you always have to be so crude? You've obviously got an extremely dirty mind."

I explained very hurriedly that the poem wasn't one of mine. "It was written by Harmony Hynde."

Lucy said, "Oh, well! Her," as if that explained everything.

I don't know what she has against Harmony. Maybe it's just that she is a boffin. I have noticed that people don't always like people that are brainy.

But Harmony can't help it! It's in her genes.

I asked Lucy if she'd like to meet me in the shopping centre again, tomorrow morning. I said, "I'll buy you another Coke."

"Mmm…" She crinkled her nose. It kills me when she does that!

"I'll buy you something to eat," I said.

"I'll think about it," she said.

I said, "When will you let me know?"

She said, "When I've thought about it. But I don't want to hang about by the Swiss Clock again."

She hasn't had to hang about! Well, only the first time, when she was waiting for Sharleen.

"We could always meet in the library," I said.

She said, "In the library? What's in the library?"

"Well… there's books," I said. "And there's a place to eat."

"There's places to eat in the shopping centre. What d'you want to go to the library for?"

I explained that I wanted to see if they'd got any

books by this author that's coming to talk to us. Jason Twelvetrees.

"You mean you're going to *read* them?" said Lucy.

"Well, I thought perhaps I ought," I said. "I mean, as he's coming." Lucy tossed her head and said, "One was bad enough."

She meant the one we did in class, with Mr Mounsey. *Doomageddon*. I thought it was quite interesting, actually. But I didn't let on. I mean, I didn't want to put her off, or anything.

I said, "So you'll let me know?"

"I told you," said Lucy. "When I've thought about it."

"Give me a ring," I said.

She's got my number. Maybe she'll ring me tomorrow.

N is for nuddy,
A word for nude.
Oh, Lucy, nuddy!
I'm not being rude.

I waited in as long as I could, but Lucy never rang me. So then I went to the library and waited there. I thought perhaps she might turn up. I thought she might have forgotten I'd said to give me a ring.

I waited for almost an hour, then the Town Hall clock struck eleven and I just knew she wasn't going to come.

I expect what it was, she didn't want to be on her own with me in case I tried to kiss her again. I can see now that I was a bit too macho last Saturday. I shouldn't have done what I did. But I'd brought my *Poem to Lucy's Cheek*, and I would have liked to give it to her. I know that she enjoys my poetry. My real poetry. Not Disgusting Ditties. It shows she has taste!

When I went through to the children's section to look for some more books by Jason Twelvetrees I found Harmony in there. She was also looking for books by Jason Twelvetrees. They only had two, so we took one each. Harmony said she was really looking forward to hearing him talk. She said she'd never met a real live writer before. I said me neither.

"He might be able to help us get our book published," said Harmony. She said she was working on some more ditties, but she hadn't finished them yet. She said, "How far have you got?"

I told her I'd got as far as N. She immediately wanted to know what N stood for.

"Oh... um! I'm not quite sure," I said. I wasn't going to tell her about Lucy in the nuddy. No way!

"I'd thought of naked," said Harmony.

I said, "Yeah. Naked would be all right."

"It's not the same as yours, is it?" she said. "We don't want to have two the same."

I said, "No, but we can have variations."

Harmony wrinkled her brow and said, "Like what?"

"Well," I said, "like... boob and breast. Or bum and bottom."

"Oh, I see what you mean," said Harmony. "Yes, that would be OK."

It suddenly occurred to me that when our book was published I would have to go through and take out every mention of Lucy's name! I would have to use a pretend one, and that would upset some of my rhymes. L is for lips, for instance. L is for lips, so soft and juicy... They would have to be something else, like –

I couldn't think of anything! All I could think of was manna.

Lovely lips
As soft as manna.
I'd love to kiss
The lips of Hannah.

Except that I don't know anything about manna. I don't even know whether it *is* soft. I said to Harmony, as we left the library, "You know manna?"

"Do I?" said Harmony.

"Manna. In the Bible."

"Oh! Yes," she said. "That manna."

"What exactly was it?" I said.

"It was the food of the Israelites in the wilderness," said Harmony. She's the sort of girl that always knows these things.

"Was it soft?" I said.

"I suppose some of it was. You probably got different types."

"Like soft roe and hard roe," I said.

I said it without thinking. Harmony narrowed her eyes.

"Sorry," I said. "I forgot you were a vegetarian."

It's not very poetic, anyway. I shall have to think of something else.

Harmony wanted to know if I was going into the shopping centre. I said, "Yes, I suppose so." I couldn't think of anything else.

She said, "What do you usually do when you come here? Do you just look at the shops?"

I said, "Only the model shop, really."

"So what do you mostly do?"

I said, "Well…" And I told her about going to the car park and setting off car alarms.

"Just as a game," I said. "We dare each other."

"Who's we?" said Harmony.

"Me and Bones."

"Aren't you scared of getting caught?"

"Part of the fun," I said.

"I'd be scared," said Harmony. And then she said, "I've got a dare game! It's something I've just invented. D'you want to hear it?"

Harmony's game was that you had to dare each other to go up to someone and ask them a question in a foreign accent. "And not giggle!" She said if you giggled, you forfeited a point.

"The person that loses most points has to buy the other one a Coke. Shall we play it?"

Well, I mean, I didn't have anything else to do.

"You go first," said Harmony.

"Why me?" I said.

"Because I say so," said Harmony. She can be very bossy. "I dare you to go up to someone and ask them where the toilet is... in a French accent!"

It was far more scary than setting off car alarms.

"Well, go on!" said Harmony. "I'm daring you!"

So I went up to this really nerdy-looking person in a raincoat and said, "Excusy, monsieur! Where, pleez, is ze toilette?"

"Ze toilette for ze man," added Harmony.

I don't know whether she was genuinely trying to be helpful or whether she was just trying to make me giggle. But anyway, I didn't!

I didn't even giggle when the person in the raincoat said he was sorry he couldn't help me, he was a foreigner. Harmony did! I told her she had forfeited a point but she said it didn't count if the other person giggled. Only the person that was asking the question. I thought that was cheating, myself, but she said that she had invented the game and she was the one that made up the rules, so to pay her out I said, "All right! I dare you to ask someone where Marks & Spencer is… in a Japanese accent!"

"Ah, so!" cried Harmony. "Mark & Spensah!"

You'd never think, to look at her, that she'd be the sort of person to play a game like that. You'd think she'd be really geeky and serious, but actually she's quite funny when you get to know her.

We went all round the shopping centre asking people things in different accents. First we did foreign ones, and when we couldn't think of any more of those we started on Welsh and Irish and stuff like that. In the end I was getting pretty hungry so I dared Harmony to go and buy us some ice pops "in a West Country accent".

She went waltzing up to this little window where they sell them and said, "Oi want a straw'bry oice pop fer 'im an' a raspb'ry oice pop fer oi."

What happened next was totally unexpected. This girl shot out of the window like a jack in the box and went, "Harmony Hynde, have you been drinking?"

It was one of the Year 12s from school! Fortunately she didn't recognise me; only Harmony. This is because (Harmony told me) she lives in the same road as her.

Harmony went "Ug! Wah!" and collapsed against me, giggling. I had to put my arms round her or she'd have fallen over. *Definitely* no more than A.

But she felt kind of nice. I just wish it had been Lucy!

We bumped into Lucy while we were eating our ice pops (which Harmony bought for us in her normal voice as she'd forfeited loads more points than me. She's just as giggly as any other girl is what it comes down to).

Lucy was with Sharleen. They were arm in arm. As usual.

"Didn't take you long to find someone else, then, did it?" said Lucy.

"Boys!" sniffed Sharleen. And they both went stalking off.

I was mortified. (I think that is the word.) I felt that Lucy would never forgive me. But since then I have had time to reflect and I think perhaps it may have been a good thing for her to see me with another girl, even if it was only Harmony. It will make her scared of losing me!

I am definitely going to give her her poem. *Poem to Lucy's Cheek*. It is a question of finding the right moment.

After she and Sharleen had gone, Harmony said, "Do you fancy her?"

Do I fancy Lucy??? That is the understatement of the year! Of the decade!! Of the century!!!

"All the boys do," said Harmony.

She sounded really wistful. It made me feel a bit sorry for her, like I did the other day. We'd had fun doing all the accents and everything. I think maybe I'll write a poem for her. Something intelligent. Something she'd appreciate.

Before we went home she said, "How about cauliflower ears?"

I suppose that could be classed as a figure of speech.

O is for off
Meaning tasteless and crude.
Filthy, disgusting,
Not to say lewd.
"That's a bit off!" my mum
                        would cry
If my ditties she could espy.

Mum is never going to espy my ditties! I think she might faint if she saw some of the things I have written. That is why I keep this book under lock and key. I wonder where Harmony keeps hers?

When it is published it will be different, because then I shall be an author. Nobody minds if an author uses bad language or has lewd thoughts.

This morning Jason Twelvetrees came to talk to us. I was very surprised when I walked into the hall and saw him perched there, on a stool. He is quite old and threadbare. Like, he was wearing this really saggy tweedy jacket and these tatty jeans with the knees all ballooning out and the bottoms all frayed.

I thought an author would be quite rich and smart, but I don't think Jason Twelvetrees can be very rich as he told us that he had to travel by train as his car had broken down. In this gloomy, graveyard voice he said, "It's not a very reliable vehicle at the best of times... it's vintage. Like me."

He is quite a lugubrious sort of person. He started off by asking, not very hopefully, how many of us actually enjoyed reading. My hand at once shot up, and so did Harmony's. Bones's sort of flapped at half-mast. Three of the girls also draped their arms in the air, though I think they only did it to score brownie points (in front of the teachers) as I have never seen any of them in the library.

So then Mr Twelvetrees asked how many people *didn't* enjoy reading. I don't think it was very wise to have done that. There was this long silence, and I saw eyes flickering to the side of the hall, where all the teachers were sitting.

"Don't be afraid to tell the truth," said Mr Twelvetrees. "I believe corporal punishment has been abolished."

Me and Harmony laughed at this. So did the teachers. One or two other people tittered, rather nervously, but I think a lot of them, probably, didn't know what corporal punishment was.

"Be honest!" said this poor foolish author. I mean, boy, was he ever asking for trouble! "How many of you positively do not like reading?"

Well! I couldn't have counted the number of hands that shot up. Kelvin Clegg put up both of his, and Stuart Sprague yelled out that he hated it. "*Hate* it!" he went. "*Hate* it!"

Poor Mr Twelvetrees looked a bit taken aback at this. He said, "Well!" and took off his glasses and pinched the bridge of his nose.

All the teachers sat there looking grave. I could see their eyes going like laser beams, ready to zap any trouble-makers.

"Well, I certainly asked for that, didn't I?" said Mr Twelvetrees.

Kelvin Clegg agreed, in his raucous Neanderthal voice, that he had. Mr Mounsey went all purple in the face and glared at him.

Fortunately, Mr Twelvetrees told us, he was a man who expected very little of life. He said, "I am not by nature what you would call an optimist. The cold winds of fortune have buffeted me. *Nil esperandum* is my motto."

Me and Harmony and some of the teachers laughed again. I mean, it was obviously a joke of some kind, so it seemed only polite. (Harmony explained it to me afterwards: "*Nil desperandum*, never despair. *Nil esperandum*, never hope." That girl knows everything!)

So anyway, old Mr Twelvetrees he starts telling us how he came to write this book called *Doomageddon* that we'd all read. I have to admit, he's not the most inspiring speaker I have ever heard as he sort of mumbles and chews on his words, and he keeps stopping every now and again to mop his brow and take sips from a glass of water, but he wasn't as boring as all that. I mean, if you actually bothered to listen to what he was saying, it was quite interesting. Only of course nobody did. Just me and Harmony.

Kelvin Clegg started a punch-up and had to be sent out. Stuart Sprague fell asleep. Some of the girls giggled. I felt really sorry for Mr Twelvetrees. He was probably sitting there thinking they were giggling at him and wondering if he'd got snot hanging out of his nose or was wearing odd shoes, or something. That's what I'd have been thinking if I'd been him.

At the end he asked if anyone had any questions. Harmony wanted to know if he could tell us how to get a book published. He said, "With immense difficulty, my dear young lady. With immense difficulty."

He said that you had to be very thick-skinned and not break down in tears every time a publisher rejected you. He said, "Swear, by all means! Swear as much as you like. But then pick yourself up and carry on."

Bones whispered to me, "I'm going to ask him something!" Bones wanted to know how much money an author earnt. I saw Mr Mounsey raise his eyes heavenwards and I knew he'd have something to say to Bones afterwards. But as Bones explained to me, "These things are important."

Anyway, Mr Twelvetrees told us that most authors don't even earn enough to live on. He said, "It is a grossly underpaid occupation. Enter it at your peril. Any more questions?"

He peered at us over his glasses, and there was this deathly hush. Some people started to look at their watches. I didn't want him to go away feeling unappreciated, so I put my hand up and said, "I'm writing a novel." Lots of people groaned, but I reckon old Mr Twelvetrees was pretty pleased because he said, "Are you, indeed? A tale of spills and thrills, no doubt?"

I said, "Well, actually, it's about the inner life of a cockroach. I could tell you how it begins, if you like. *I am a cockroach. I live in dark places, shunning the light. I am a lowly creature, vilified by all.*"

It is a good word, vilified. I hope Mr Mounsey was listening. He is always saying how we should extend our vocabularies.

I told Mr Twelvetrees the whole story of *Cockroach*. Well, almost the whole story. I'd just got to the part where the exterminators come with their exterminating gear when Mr Mounsey said, "This is fascinating, Salvatore, but I think we shall have to call it a day."

It was a pity he stopped me, as the next bit is really exciting.

Mr Twelvetrees thanked me quite profusely. He said that he would really like to read the book when I have finished it.

I almost have! I am going to finish it tonight and send him a copy.

All the time I was telling my cockroach story I could see Lucy, turned round in her seat, looking at me like she just couldn't believe it. I found that very encouraging. At lunch time, in the canteen, I managed to get in the queue just behind her.

"Well, look who it isn't!" she said. "Mr Cockroach himself!"

I told her that I had something for her. She said, "What is it this time?"

I handed her the sealed envelope in which I had placed her poem and hissed, "Read this when you are alone!"

"Not more?" cried Lucy.

She was definitely impressed!

P is for pimples, in other words, spots,
Of which adolescents can have lots.
A spot on the bum is a right royal pain,
So's a spot on the conk if you're
                        someone that's vain.
Spots, however, can be fun!
You can burst them, one by one.
This is how to burst a spot:
First you squeeze, and then you pop.
The head flies out — ping, thunk, plop!
After which there comes a gush
Of utterly disgusting mush.

Getting rid of putrefaction
Gives a lot of satisfaction.

I have come to the conclusion that picking spots is all
the satisfaction I am ever likely to get. My life is a
disaster. I asked Lucy if she'd like to meet me this
Saturday, anywhere she chose. She said, "Get a life,
Tomato! You are just so sad! You know that? You are
just *so sad*!"

She said she'd had enough of me hanging around after her. She said I was a stuck-up twit, "droning on about your stupid cockroaches," and that if I thought saying someone's cheek was squishy was poetic, I must be out of my mind.

She said, "Why don't you do us all a favour? Dig a hole and bury yourself!"

And then as she flounced off she hurled the word "Cockroach!" at me over her shoulder.

I can't think what I have done to upset her. What is wrong with the word squishy? Lucy's cheeks are soft and squishy, Other people's cheeks are fishy. You'd think she'd see that it was intended as a compliment.

And why did she say I was stuck up? Just because I told Jason Twelvetrees about *I Am A Cockroach*! I don't understand it.

I obviously have a long way to go before I unravel the mystery of the opposite sex. But I do know that the path of true love never runs smoothly, so I do not intend to despair. What it probably means is that she fancies me like crazy but is too scared to commit herself. I must be patient with her.

Right now I shall follow my intellectual pursuits. For example, I have finished *Cockroach*. The last words of the book are the same as the first:

I am a cockroach. I live in dark places, shunning the light.

I have done this deliberately, so the reader will feel that he* has come full circle. I wonder if it is possible to make a book in segments, like an orange?

This would be ideal! A circular book!

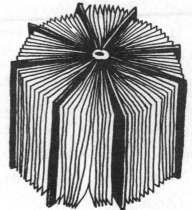

I have sent a copy to Mr Twelvetrees. (Me and Harmony both asked him for his address.) This is the letter that I wrote to go with it:

---

* I realise I should have said he or she. I would not like Harmony to accuse me of being sexist.

Dear Mr Twelvetrees,

I very much enjoyed your visit to my school this week and feel that I have learnt a great deal from it.

The things that I have mainly learnt are:

a) an author must not burst into tears when a publisher does not want to publish their book

b) authors do not earn very much money and

c) people become authors at their peril.

I have considered this last point very carefully, but I feel that in this life you have to be prepared to take risks and so I have decided that an author is what I am going to be.

I am sending you a copy of my book, 'I Am A Cockroach', that I told you about. I should be most grateful if you would read it and tell me whether you consider it is good enough to be published, and if so please could you give me the names of some publishers.

I am waiting eagerly to hear from you.

Yours very sincerely,

(signed) Salvatore d'Amato

P.S. I realise you must be extremely busy writing your own books, but I would like you to know that your talk inspired me tremendously.

This last bit was not strictly true but I felt he needed all the encouragement he could get. I felt that it was quite brave of him to stand up and try to talk about books in front of people such as Kelvin Clegg, although I expect he didn't have much choice as he probably needed the money for getting his car repaired. Before he left I heard him asking Mr Mounsey whether his cheque was ready. I hope it was. I think he deserved it.

Harmony says that she has also written to Mr Twelvetrees. She has also sent him a book! She said, "It's about the Great Wall of China in the 5th Century. I've done fifty pages so far. There are going to be more than five hundred when I've finished."

I was amazed. *I Am A Cockroach* only has forty-six! I told this to Harmony and she said it was obviously a novella rather than a novel.

I said, "What's a novella?"

"A little novel," said Harmony.

It didn't seem little while I was writing it. I hope it isn't too short!

As well as finishing *Cockroach* and writing to Mr Twelvetrees I have also started on a poem for Harmony.

Harmony Hynde,
I love your mind.

That is as far as I have got. I shall add to it as more ideas come to me. I am waiting for inspiration. Here is another figure of speech: over the moon.

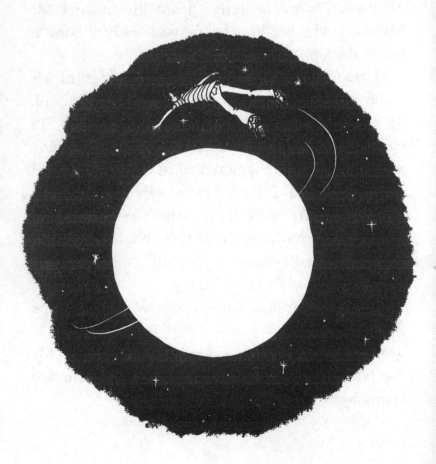

Q is a letter that's followed by U
And that is the best that I can do.

Met Harmony at the library. We were both taking our Jason Twelvetrees back.

"I can't think of anything for Q," I said. "Can you?"

Harmony said she hadn't got as far as Q. She said, "Why don't we go and have a pizza and I'll think about it? Unless you're meeting Lucy," she added.

Just for a minute I felt a glow. Because if Harmony reckons that me and Lucy are going out together, other people must, too! But then I remembered that Lucy had told me to dig a hole and bury myself, and I came over all glum and said, "No, I'm not meeting her."

We went to the Caromon Cafe that's in the library and bought a couple of pizzas and sort of got talking about things. I told Harmony about my sister, about how she's got Tourette's and how I was worried in case I might get it.

Harmony said, "Is Tourette's that thing where you can't stop swearing?"

"Yes," I said. "Four-letter words just come spewing out of you before you can stop them."

"So what are you worried about?" said Harmony. "It sounds like fun!"

She told me how in her road there was this sweet old lady, very respectable, who shouted swear words at car drivers when they cut her up. She said, "I'm going to do that when I'm old."

I said, "It's all right to do it when you're old. They don't get mad at you like they do when you're young."

Harmony said, "That's true."

I then told her how I hated my name. I said that

parents did these terrible things to their children without ever stopping to think.

"I mean," I said, "*Salvatore*."

"But it's Italian," said Harmony. "It's nice!"

I said she wouldn't think it was nice if she was a boy and kept being called Sally.

"It was Mum," I said. "Going through her Italian phase."

"Going back to her roots," said Harmony.

"It's not her roots!"

"Well, your dad's."

I said, "My dad doesn't even speak Italian! His name isn't even Italian. He's called Jake!" And I told her how Dad's great great grandad had come to this country in *1885*, for goodness' sake!

That shut her up a bit. Just for a few seconds.

"It's still a good name," she said. "Not like mine. Imagine what it's like being called Harmony!"

I'd never thought about that. Harmony told me that her parents were seriously unbalanced. She said that she had two sisters, a younger one that was called Viola, pronounced VeeOla, and an older one that was called Melody.

She said, "They did it because they're music freaks."

She said that everyone in her family played a

musical instrument. Her mum plays the cello, her dad plays the clarinet, VeeOla plays – the veeola! Melody plays the piano and Harmony plays the violin.

"Honestly," she said, "it's a cacophony."

I said, "What do you think they'd have called a boy?"

Harmony rolled her eyes and said, "Sax? Tuba? Tuba Hynde!"

"It's criminal," I said. "It shouldn't be allowed."

"Did you know," said Harmony, "that there was once a couple that christened their baby Thingie?"

I said, "*Thingie?*" and we both collapsed.

"You see, it could be worse," said Harmony. And then she said, "I've thought of something for Q! How about, Q is for quart, Which rhymes with wart? Or else you could have, Q is for queen, Which rhymes with obscene. Or, Q is for queer, Which rhymes with leer."

It never occurred to me to do that. I said, "I kept trying to think of rude words that began with Q!"

"I don't think there are any," said Harmony. "It's not a very rude sort of letter." Then all nonchalant she goes, "By the way, I've bought you a present. Here!"

And she thrust this tatty old brown envelope at me. Inside the envelope was – a copy of Brewer's! Brewer's Dictionary of Phrase and Fable.

"I'm afraid it's only second-hand," she said. "But I thought you might like it."

I said, "That's great!" It is, too. I keep breaking off to look things up in it. It's what Mr Mounsey would call a mine of information. Inside, she's written "For Salvatore with love from Harmony". (I only noticed that when I got back home.)

"I was hoping I'd bump into you," she said, "so that I could give it to you."

I said, "Hey, wow, thanks, Harmony!" and she looked really pleased. I told her that I'd got a present for her. "Only I haven't finished it yet... it's a poem I'm writing for you."

"For me?" squeaked Harmony; and her face turned this sort of pale rose-pink. It made her look quite prettyish. Not as pretty as Lucy, of course! No one could look as pretty as Lucy.

Luscious Lucy, so divine!
Lucy, please won't you be mine?

I can't stop thinking about her! My hormones must be in a terrible state. I picture them as being these little self-important blobby things with legs, frantically dashing about in my blood stream.

Harmony wanted to know what sort of poem I was writing. She said, "Is it a disgusting one?"

I said, "No, of course it's not."

She said, "Is it a funny one?"

"No," I said. "It's a serious one." And then

quickly, before she could go getting the wrong idea, I said, "But it's not yucky."

"You mean, it's not a love poem," said Harmony.

"Well – um – no," I said, "not exactly."

"It's all right," said Harmony. "I wouldn't expect you to write me a love poem. That's more the sort of thing you'd write for Lucy."

When she said the name Lucy, all my hormones rushed to my face and started yammering to get out. It was like I was on fire! Harmony looked at me, sympathetically.

"Does it hurt?" she said.

I said, "Does w-w-what hurt?"

"Being in love," said Harmony.

I said, "I'm n-n-n-n—"

Harmony rested her elbow on the table, her chin on her hand, and leaned towards me.

"Tell me about it," she said.

I said, "I c-c-c-c—"

"Yes, you can!" she said. "You can tell me anything. We're friends!"

I said, "B-b-b-b-b—"

"Take a deep breath," said Harmony. "Now, what's the problem?"

"She t-t-told me t-t-t-to d-d-dig a hole and b-b-bury myself!" I said.

"You think she doesn't like you?"

"W-well, w-wouldn't y-you?" I said. "If s-someone t-told you to d-dig a hole and b-bury yourself?"

"It would depend who it was," said Harmony. "It could be that she's really mad about you and is just doing it to inflame your passion."

"Do you think so?" I said. I didn't mean to sound eager. But it's exactly what I'd been thinking!

"Well, it could be," said Harmony. "I mean, I couldn't say for certain."

How am I to find out? This is the question!

"I don't expect," said Harmony, in matter of fact tones, "that anyone will ever be inflamed by me."

"Why not?" I said.

"Glasses," said Harmony, "for one thing. Teeth," she said, "for another." Hair," she said, "for another."

"I'm sure that someone will love you for your mind," I said.

Harmony said she supposed she would have to be content with that.

I felt deeply moved and have now written four more lines of her poem:

Harmony Hynde
I love your mind!
The way you read books —
More important than looks!
The way that you talk —
Who cares how you walk?

I have noticed that when Lucy walks she goes bibbity bobbity, bibbity bobbity, with her bum bouncing up and down. Harmony's bum doesn't do that. She doesn't really have one. But I do admire her mind!

R is for rear,
For rump or for bum.
Stand in the playground
and see them come!
Big bums, small bums,
Hardly there at all bums!
Bums that wobble,
Bums that pobble,
Bums in trousers,
Bums on bikes,
Bums of every
Size and type.
But the bum that I like best
Is the bum of Lucy West!

She is still pretending not to fancy me. I don't know whether she wants me to throw myself at her, or what. Maybe I should act like I am attracted to someone else? Harmony, for example.

I am not sure whether she would be inflamed by seeing me with Harmony, but just at the moment

Harmony is the only girl who will have anything to do with me. I seem to have upset everyone by telling Jason Twelvetrees about my *Cockroach* book. They keep calling me Cockroach, or Boff. Carrie Pringle accused me of being something that lives in sewers. I thought that was quite unnecessary. Why am I so misunderstood?

My sister has been especially unpleasant to me. She said I was a sad little pervert, stinking up her way of life. This is because she discovered that I had used her foaming face cleanser again. I didn't use that much!

And how does she know, anyway? Unless she has been spying on me?

I am feeling very depressed. I only have eight more letters to go and Lucy, my Lucy, the light of my life! She shows no sign of warming towards me. What must I do to win her love???

I feel more than ever in sympathy with cockroaches. If I thought they would respond to the human touch, I would keep one as a pet.

S is for sex
Which is on my brain.
I think of Lucy
Again and again!

Today in the library, Harmony asked me about my
cockroach story. She said, "I really like the sound of
it! It sounds really good."

I said, "You could read it if you like. The trouble
is, I've only got one copy. I sent the other to Jason
Twelvetrees."

"Yes, and if our house burnt down and the other
one got lost in the post, it would be a disaster," agreed
Harmony. "You shouldn't ever lend your only copy."

"This is it," I said. And then before I could do
anything to stop it my mouth had gone and opened
all of its own accord and blurted out, "You could
always come round and have a read of it at my
place!"

I don't know why it said that. It was like it has
this mind of its own. I mean, I knew what would
happen if my sister saw me with Harmony.

"Sally's got a girlfriend, Sally's got a girlfriend!"

On the other hand, I did quite enjoy the idea of Harmony reading my book. She'd be the first person to do so!

"When shall I come?" she said. She was dead keen!

"Well, I suppose you could come today if you wanted," I said.

"After school?" She beamed at me; this big toothy beam. She looks really goofy when she does that! But I quite like it. So I said yes, after school would be fine, and that is what we agreed.

Lucy has been ignoring me all week. I know it's because I said her lips were squishy. I have been trying desperately to think of something else they could be... plump and juicy? Round and rosy? I will have to put my mind to it.

As well as thinking of words to describe Lucy's cheek I have been looking for an opportunity to inflame her passion. That opportunity came today! At half-past three, as me and Harmony were going out of the school gates, we found ourselves on a collision course with... guess who? Lucy and

Sharleen! I didn't hesitate. I knew I had to act fast, so I immediately seized hold of Harmony's hand. I think Harmony was a bit surprised, but she didn't seem to mind.

Unfortunately, neither did Lucy. She just smirked and said, "Nice day for it!" Then she and Sharleen shrieked with laughter. Sharleen hissed, "Cockroach!"

"Such tiny little shrunken minds," said Harmony.

But it's not Lucy's mind that I fancy. It's her body!!!

As soon as the two of them had gone wobbling off, I tried to get my hand back but Harmony seemed to have it in a vice-like grip. I didn't like to start struggling, I mean it wouldn't have looked very manly, so in the end I was forced to leave it there. It felt OK. Quite nice, really.

This is the first time I have pressed flesh. So I suppose, in a way, it is a landmark.

When we got home my sister was out. Deep relief. I grabbed some milk and a packet of biscuits and took Harmony up to my room. We sat on the bed and I read her all forty-six pages of *I Am A*

Cockroach. While I was reading it she ate most of
the biscuits, for which she apologised afterwards.

She said, "I got so carried away listening, I didn't
realise what I was doing."

I said that was OK as I wasn't particularly hungry.
But if she always eats like that I don't know how she
stays so sticklike!

"What did you think of the book?" I said. "Please be ruthlessly honest."

"Right. Well. Being ruthlessly honest," said Harmony.

She paused. I said, "Yes?"

"Being ruthlessly honest," she said, "I thought it was brilliant!"

"Really?" I said.

I wanted to make sure. She may not be the object of my passion, but I value her opinion.

"Really and truly!" said Harmony. "I really liked it. Usually when boys write anything it's all fighting and violence."

"There is *some* violence," I said. "The bit where they try to squash him with a shoe."

"Yes, but that's only one small incident. Mostly," said Harmony, "it's what I'd call psychological… full of insight."

"Well," I said, trying to sound modest, "that was my aim. My aim was to get inside the mind of a cockroach."

"Which you did! Perfectly! I shall never look at cockroaches the same way again," said Harmony. "Not," she added, "being ruthlessly honest, that I have ever actually seen one."

"Me neither," I said.

Harmony said that made it all the more amazing that I could actually pretend to be one. I suppose it does.

"Do you feel that you relate to cockroaches?" said Harmony. "Do you feel an affinity with them?"

I said that I did, and she nodded and said, "Yes, I thought you must. It comes across."

So then I told her – I don't know why – about how at one time I had thought there was something wrong with me. I told her that I had even been scared I might be gay. She cried, "But there's nothing to be ashamed of in being gay!"

"Well – no," I said, "but I'm glad I'm not."

"Why are you glad?" demanded Harmony.

"Well, if I was, I wouldn't fancy girls!" I said.

"You mean, you wouldn't fancy Lucy West," said Harmony.

It is very unsettling, the way Harmony can get into my brain and read what I am thinking. I asked her (later on, so's she wouldn't guess it was anything to do with Lucy) if she reckoned it was an insult to describe someone's cheek as being squishy. She gave this great screech of laughter and said, "You have to be joking!"

I said, "I am not joking. I am in deathly earnest."

Harmony said, "OK, and I am being ruthlessly

honest." She said that squishy was not a good word to use for a cheek.

I said, "So what would be a good word, do you think?"

But Harmony just cackled and said, "I'm not writing your love lyrics for you! Think of one yourself!"

This is what I have thought of so far:

1. Lucy's cheek is soft and round
   Like a beach ball it would bound.
2. Lucy's cheek is soft and pink
   Of a peach it makes one think.
3. Lucy's cheek is ruby red
   As if on strawberries she's fed.
4. Lucy's cheek is pink and pouchy
   Lucy never could look grouchy!

None of them seem quite right. But I have added two more lines to Harmony's poem:

Never mind your flattened chest
Your brain is ace - by far the best!

I think she would like that.

T is for tit,
Both a bird and a breast.
I know which one
That I like best!

I have discovered that Harmony isn't even an A. She's nothing at all! I asked her and she told me. Harmony and me can talk of things like breasts. She's amazing that way. I think she could teach me quite a lot about girls.

I would have thought, for instance, that she would find it very worrying and upsetting not even to be an A. Like if I was a girl and didn't have a bosom I would immediately imagine there was something wrong with me. I would probably start fantasising that I had been born into the wrong body and was really meant to be a boy. But Harmony says the longer she can go without having a bosom, the better it will be as far as she is concerned.

"After all," she said, "what use would it be?"

I said, "Well, I suppose if it was big enough you could balance things on it."

"You mean, use it like a sort of shelf?" said Harmony.

At that we got a bit silly and started thinking up all the ways that a bosom could come in useful. Like, for instance, you could hang things on it.

You could open doors with it.

You could strike muggers with it.

You could scatter crowds with it.

But Harmony said she still didn't want one.

I think perhaps, in spite of having this mega-sized brain, she is still a bit immature. I like the thought that in this respect I am ahead of her. My hormones are raging like crazy! I reckon Harmony's are still asleep.

I don't know how we got talking about boobs and breasts and busts and bosoms. We started off talking about Jason Twelvetrees. He has written to us! Both of us. This is his letter to me:

Dear **Salvatore**,

Thank you so much for your lovely letter. It was most kind of you to write.

I have read your book 'I Am A Cockroach' and very much enjoyed it. I think, to be published, it would need to be a little longer – another half dozen chapters, say – but it is certainly very promising. I wish you all the best with it.

I am glad my talk inspired you. I am enclosing a list of books that I have written. Maybe you will be able to find them in your local bookshop.

All good wishes,

Jason Twelvetrees

P.S. You may be interested to know that I shall be appearing in Waterstone's book store in the Burnett Centre this Saturday at 12 noon.

This was Harmony's one:

Dear **Harmony**,

Thank you so much for your lovely letter. It was most kind of you to write.

I have read your book 'The Great Wall of China' and very much enjoyed it. I think, to be published, it would need to be a little longer – another half dozen chapters, say – but it is certainly very promising. I wish you all the best with it.

I am glad my talk inspired you. I am enclosing a list of books that I have written. Maybe you will be able to find them in your local bookshop.

All good wishes,

Jason Twelvetrees

P.S. You may be interested to know that I shall be appearing in Waterstone's book store in the Burnett Centre this Saturday at 12 noon.

We sat in the library together at lunch time and pored over our letters.

"I did tell him," said Harmony, "that my book wasn't finished."

"He's pretty old," I said. "Maybe he forgot."

"Mm. Maybe," said Harmony.

We studied the letters side by side.

I said, "It's good he wrote our names by hand… it makes them more personal."

"And different," said Harmony.

We agreed that Jason Twelvetrees probably has millions of fan letters and that it was pretty good that he bothered to reply at all.

We also agreed that we would go to see him in Waterstone's on Saturday morning.

"It's bound to be crowded out," said Harmony, "but we might at least be able to say hello."

She asked me how her poem was coming along. I said that I was still working on it.

"It must be a really long one!" she said.

She sounded quite excited. She then told me another figure of speech she'd found: all fingers and thumbs.

U is for ugh!
A noise of distaste.
Like Ugh! Poo!
Doggy do!
Ugh! Pox!
Sweaty socks!
Ugh! Yuck!
A pile of muck!
Bad eggs and drains can also smell
So can cheesy feet, as well.

Best thing to do,
ALWAYS CARRY
A CLOTHES PEG.

Well! Jason Twelvetrees didn't smell of cheesy feet but his breath was a bit pongy. It smelt like something had died. Harmony reckons it's because he smokes.

We didn't get to Waterstone's until quarter past twelve. We thought there would be this great long queue snaking out the door and half way round the shopping centre, but all we saw, when we reached the children's department, was Jason Twelvetrees sitting mournfully at a table behind a pile of books.

His books. Ones he had written. I think maybe he was hoping to sell them.

He looked up with quite an optimistic expression when me and Harmony arrived.

"And what can I do for you?" he said, reaching for his pen. "Have you chosen your books?"

We hadn't really gone there to buy books; just to say hallo and thank him for his letters. It was obvious he didn't recognise us, but as Harmony said afterwards, he probably meets too many people to remember all of them.

"You came to our school," I reminded him.

"We wrote to you," said Harmony. "We sent you our stories."

"Ah! Did you?" he said; and the optimistic expression began to fade. "Did I reply?"

"Yes, you did," said Harmony.

"Oh, well, that's good," he said. "You haven't come to tick me off."

We stood there a while, just to keep him company really, until some more people arrived. But all that happened was this woman came up and asked him where the Roald Dahls were. After a bit we got to feeling sorry for him, all bald and threadbare, sitting there trying to look as if he wasn't really interested in people buying his books. Like he was just there for show, or to pass the time of day or something. So what we did, we both bought one. I bought one called *Jampot Jane* and Harmony bought one called *Mr Munch the Lunch Box Man*.

Mr Twelvetrees said, "You realise these are way too young for you? These are meant for five-year-olds."

They just happened to be the cheapest. I mumbled that I couldn't afford one of the bigger ones.

Harmony said brightly that she was buying *Mr Munch* for her little sister. (Who I happen to know is ten years old and some kind of child genius.)

Mr Twelvetrees seemed resigned. He said, "Ah, well! So be it," and wrote *Best wishes Jason Twelvetrees* in his spidery old handwriting inside the covers.

Best Wishes
Jason Twelvetrees

Just as we were going, a little kid came up to him clutching a Goosebumps which he wanted him to sign. Old Jason Twelvetrees got quite snotty. He snapped, "Now why would you expect me to sign something which I did not write?"

The little kid looked quite crestfallen. He probably thought one author was the same as any other author. I reckon it wouldn't have hurt Mr Twelvetrees to sign his Goosebumps for him.

"What shall we do with these?" I said to Harmony, once we were outside. I meant *Jampot Jane* and *Mr Munch*.

"Keep 'em!" said Harmony. "Signed copies... could be valuable." And then she confessed that she could have afforded one of the more expensive ones, but that Jason Twelvetrees didn't really write her sort of book.

I asked her what her sort of book was and she said that just at the moment she was reading *Pride and Prejudice*.

"By Jane Austen," she said.

I said, "I know who it's by!"

I must be honest, however. With myself, I mean. Sometimes you try to hoodwink yourself. I have to admit that last term I'd never even heard of Jane Austen. Mr Mounsey was giving us a quiz in one of our English lessons, all about books and authors. When he asked if anyone knew who Jane Austen was, old Lucy stuck her hand up and said, "She's a tennis player."

Well, she could have been, for all I knew. Except I didn't really see why Mr Mounsey would be talking about tennis players in an English lesson.

I reminded Harmony of this, and she gave a happy cackle. (She was the only one who'd known.)

"She's a sex object," said Harmony.

"Who? Jane Austen?" I said.

"No! Dummy!" She biffed me with her *Mr Munch* book. "Lucy West!"

"Can't you be a sex object *and* know about Jane Austen?" I said.

Harmony said, "Well, she didn't!"

I had this feeling that I was being unloyal. To Lucy, I mean. (I think maybe that word should be disloyal.) I also wasn't sure that you were supposed to describe girls as sex objects. I said to Harmony, "That's not very P.C."

"So what? I wouldn't mind being one," said Harmony.

I said, "You?" I was kind of, like, a bit gobsmacked to tell the truth. "But you'd have to have a bosom!" I said.

Harmony sighed and agreed that that was probably true.

Well, it is! You can't be a sex object without a bosom. Stands to reason.

All the same, I was quite surprised.

Before we said goodbye, Harmony asked me yet again about her poem.

"Is it nearly finished? I'm dying to read it!"

I told her I was revising it. I'm a bit worried, now. Now that I know she nurses this secret desire to be a sex object. I might have to re-write it!

V is for vulgar,
Which is what I have been.
Verging occasionally
On the obscene.

I am beginning to grow bored of keeping this alphabet. There is obviously something drastically wrong with me. I am doomed to failure. I shall end up as a weird crusty bachelor whom nobody loves. Everyone will shun me and hold me in contempt. I shall be a human version of a cockroach.

Today I tried to give Lucy her new poem, *Poem to Lucy's Cheek*. I said, "It's different! I've revised it."

She said, "Piss off, Tomato! I can do without any more so-called poetry, thank you very much."

"But you'll like this version," I said. "It's a new one!"

Lucy screeched, "Go jump in a pool of snot!" Then she snatched the poem out of my hands, screwed it into a ball and hurled it viciously into the road, where it got run over by a bus. I felt very disheartened and wondered to myself, what is the point of going on?

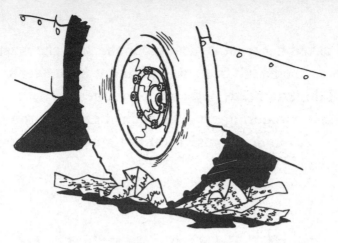

It was a good poem, too. Fortunately I can still remember it:

> Lucy's cheek is softly pink,
> Of strawberries it makes me think.
> She has dimples when she beams!
> Of Lucy's cheek I could write reams.
> But I will only say one thing:
> Let us all to Lucy sing!

How could she possibly take exception to that? She would have loved it, I know she would! Any girl would. They wouldn't be able to help it.

I think I shall post it to her.

Harmony has given me another phrase: to nurse vipers in your bosom. She said, "It was talking about bosoms that made me think of it."

I asked her what it meant, but she said she wasn't sure as she hadn't been able to find it in Brewer's.

"I think it means harbouring grudges."

I am harbouring grudges against Lucy. Throwing my poem under a bus! I am not sure if I can ever forgive her for that.

W stands for willy,
Both childish and silly.
There's another word, so I have heard,
Which is really quite a riddle.
In the U.S. of A., or so they say,
When people want to piddle,
Their Johnson is the thing they use.
A bit of a strange word to choose.
Poor old Johnson! Who was he?
Now he's rude as rude can be.

This Disgusting Ditty was composed by Harmony. She has rushed through her alphabet at fantastic speed. She asked me if I had done one for W. I said that I hadn't. I almost said that I wasn't going to bother. I am doomed to failure and that is all there is to it. I only have three more letters to go and then I might just as well end it all.

When I say *end it*, I mean cutting myself off in my prime.

Here lies Salvatore d'Amato
Otherwise known as Sally Tomato.
Couldn't kiss a girl no matter how he tried,
So in the end, he upped and died.

"I've done two," said Harmony. "You can have one of mine, if you like. It'd be a pity to waste it."

Her other one is W for womb.

W is for womb
A little room
Where babies live and grow.

Etc. Etc. It goes on for about twenty verses. All about babies. Babies burping, babies blurting, babies being sick, babies doing things in their nappies. She said I could have that one if I wanted but I said it would take too long to copy out. She said, "I thought you'd probably prefer the willy one. Boys always snigger at the word willy."

"I didn't snigger," I said.

Harmony said that was only because I was suffering the pangs of unrequited love.

"Nothing seems funny when you're in that state."

How would she know? I bet she's never suffered!

There is only one small glimmer of hope on the

horizon. Emma Crick has invited me to her end-of-term party. She's invited Harmony, as well.

"She's probably only invited me," said Harmony, "because she wants you to go. She knows we're friends. She probably didn't think you'd go if she hadn't invited me. She probably fancies you," she added.

Can this be true??? Emma Crick was one of the girls who put their hands up when Jason Twelvetrees asked how many people enjoyed reading. Maybe she wasn't trying to impress the teachers. Maybe it was me!

The really important thing, however, is that Lucy will be there. She is still the object of my affections in spite of throwing my poem under a bus. And if I cannot get to kiss her at a party, then that is the end. I shall no longer want to go on living.

Another expression for being dead is, pushing up the daisies.

X marks the spot
While Y is for yessssss!
Z is for zenith –
The high point, no less!

I've done it, I've done it, I've kissed a girl! I'm normal! Yippeee!

Now I don't have to go out and kill myself, which is just as well as it would have been extremely inconvenient for Mum and Dad. Dad would have had to take time off to attend my funeral and Mum would have had to go out and buy herself a black dress. Also, I expect they might have missed me. My sister wouldn't, she'd probably have just been glad that I couldn't get my hands on her foaming face gel any more. But Mum would have cried, and she doesn't like doing that as it makes her eyes swell up. So it's all for the best.

It's all for the best,
I've passed the test!

I can't stop thinking in lines of poetry. I thought of some more just now.

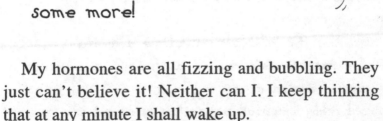

If I'd bitten the dust,
Mum would have been
fussed.
Just as well!
Saved by the bell!
I've kissed until my lips
are sore,
And now I want to do
   some more!

My hormones are all fizzing and bubbling. They just can't believe it! Neither can I. I keep thinking that at any minute I shall wake up.

This is the way that it happened. On Friday we finished term. On Saturday, which was yesterday, Emma Crick had her party.

I only went because I'd said I'd go and because in any case I didn't have anything else to do, but I wasn't feeling very hopeful. On Wednesday I sent Lucy her poem, *Poem to Lucy's Cheek*, Version II. I sent it First Class so I knew by Friday she must have got it for sure. I kept giving her these really meaningful looks, but she never responded. I didn't like to ask her outright. She might have hit me. She's only small, but she can pack quite a punch. I once saw her bash Kelvin Clegg so hard she nearly knocked him out. I didn't want that happening to me.

By Saturday I thought I'd better start making my Will. I left most everything to Mum and Dad, except for my books, which I left to Harmony. I reckoned she was the only person I knew that would properly appreciate them.

This is my Will that I wrote:

This is the Will of Salvatore d'Amato
hereinafter referred to as I, being the person
above named in this my Will
I hereby leave all my property except for my
books to my parents in loving memory
I hereby leave all my books to my good friend
Harmony Hynde
Signed this day by the said named
Salvatore d'Amato.

Immediately I'd done it I had an afterthought so I added this thing called a Codicil, meaning an afterthought to a Will.

This is a Codicil to the Will of Salvatore d'Amato therein referred to as I, being the person named in the aforesaid Will

All my Will stays the same except that to my sister Isabella I hereby leave all my underpants.

I put that in to pay her out for calling me a pervert.

It's a pity, in a way, that it never happened. I would have liked to see her face when she heard about the underpants.

Except of course that I wouldn't have been able to see as I would have been dead. And now I'm glad that I am not. Life is brilliant! Life is worth living!

But I think Harmony got it wrong about Emma fancying me. She never gave any signs of it. I think she fancies Bones, speaking personally.

I also think that Harmony ought to stop putting herself down all the time. I am going to tell her this. What makes her think she was only invited to Emma's party because Emma wanted me to come? She was obviously invited because she is a good person to have at a party. Anybody, I should think, would want Harmony to come to their party. I would!

Lucy was there, with Sharleen. Sharleen's lip curled when she saw me. She said, "Oh, Luce, look what the cat's brought in!" But Lucy smiled at me, she actually smiled. She said, "Version II was a whole lot better than Version I." So that was encouraging, for a start.

Then later, Emma said she'd got this game we'd all got to play. She said she'd played it at her cousin's party and it was fun. She said what you did, all the girls put blindfolds on and stood in a row, while the boys went outside and came back in one at a time, also wearing blindfolds, and kissed each of the girls in turn.

A really dim nerd of a boy called Alaric Prosser (which is a pretty dim and nerdy sort of name) wanted to know what the point was. Bones yelled, "If you don't know, I can't tell you!" But Emma said what the point was, it was to make a note in your mind which girl you most enjoyed kissing; or if you were a girl, which boy you most enjoyed being kissed by.

Alaric, in his dumb fashion, said, "How can you tell? If you're blindfolded?"

"You count," said Emma. "Girl no. 1, girl no. 2… there's only six of us!"

Only six!!! Me and Bones looked at each other. Bones said afterwards it was a pity Nasreen Flynn was one of them, as he'd already done her. Harmony wanted to know what happened at the end: "How do you know who was which number?"

Emma said that at the end all the boys had to line up in the same order as they'd kissed, and all the girls removed their blindfolds. Then we'd know!

The girls were: Harmony, Nasreen, Emma, Lucy, Sharleen and Carrie Pringle. I didn't know what order they were going to stand in, but I reckoned I'd know which one was Lucy all right!

When it came to my turn my hormones were raging so furiously I felt like I was about to burst into flames. Six girls all in one go! Well, almost.

No. 1 was pretty good. I thought that might be Nasreen. No. 2 was a bit prissy and prunelike. I reckoned that was probably Sharleen. No. 3 was like a piece of dead fish. Carrie Pringle, for sure. No. 4 was OK. No. 5 was so-so. No. 6 –

No. 6 was bliss! No. 6 was heaven on earth! No. 6 had got to be Lucy!

Well. When we all lined up and saw who we'd been kissing…

No. 3 was Lucy! Piece of dead fish. No. 1 was Carrie Pringle. No. 6 was... Harmony!

Life will never be the same again!!!

She rang me this morning. My sister screeched, "Salleeeeeeeeeeeeee! Your girlfriend!"

I think she is. She is my girlfriend!

We talked about the party. Harmony wanted to know what it had felt like, kissing everyone.

"Tell me who was good and who wasn't!"

I said, "Well, Carrie Pringle was OK. Nasreen was OK. Sharleen was OK. Emma was OK. Lucy was—" I hesitated here. "She was OK," I said.

"So nobody was very exciting?" said Harmony.

"Only one person," I said. "What about you? Did you find anyone exciting?"

"Only one person," said Harmony.

Then there was this pause. And then I said, "I'll tell you, if you'll tell me."

So we told each other. And now I've had to re-write my poem!

Poem for Harmony

Sweet Harmony Hynde,
I love your mind.
I love your body, too.
Your lips
When we kiss
Are utter bliss!
I'm deep in love with you!

I hope she likes it.